APRIL IN LOVE

APRIL
IN LOVE

LAURIE B. CLIFFORD

TYNDALE HOUSE PUBLISHERS, INC.
WHEATON, ILLINOIS

First printing, September 1986

Library of Congress Catalog Card Number 86-50536
ISBN 0-8423-0023-6

To Cynthia
With Love

CHAPTER
ONE

April Pennington sat on the sloping front lawn of King's College and watched a man with a salt-and-pepper beard leave his car and cross the gravel road to Hadley Hall, the administration building. "He coaches baseball," she said in the whisper-voice she reserved for solitary conversations. "Probaby high school."

Something about his lean build, the spring in his walk, and the easy way he carried himself made her give him an athletic occupation. "And married. One child. No, two. Maybe one on the way." The gray in his beard betrayed all this to her.

The double doors of Hadley Hall closed behind the object of her curiosity, and she turned to study his car. "Of course." She smiled complacently. "A station wagon. He lives in Los Lobos." She could picture his house already—a two-story Spanish stucco. His wife would have the other car at the supermarket. It would be a late model Toyota.

"I wonder why she didn't take the station wagon? It would be much easier to load than the Toyota." She lifted her face to the sun and laughed. "Poor folks trying to run their lives without me. How do they manage?"

Then, pleased by her momentary flight of fancy, she picked up the brown clipboard beside her and returned to the assignment she'd given herself for this first afternoon of spring break. After a fond greeting to her vacationing parents in Europe, she launched into her letter:

I've given myself the entire afternoon to write you. That's because I intend to write a book. So, if you don't hear from me for the rest of spring break, don't worry. You'll know how busy I am. . . .

She adjusted the green backrest, moved the clipboard from one knee to the other, and continued:

Last time I wrote I told you I'd be at Aunt Clara's for the holidays, but I'm not. I'm here on campus. You won't believe it when I tell you what happened. I'm not sure why, but on Thursday Susie Johnson just packed up her things and went home. So what could the poor professor do? He has a big project to work on over spring break. Susie had promised to stay and help, and now she's gone!

In her excitement over the news, April slid the pen tip off the paper, bounced it onto her bare leg, and left a stray blue mark just above her knee. She licked her fingertip and rubbed away the ink, then set the clipboard back down on the grass.

She filled her lungs with the ocean breeze that rolls over the central California coast and sighed deeply. She had thought it would help to get her feelings out on paper, would quiet the buzzing that had taken over her senses. "But it's not helping at all," she whispered as she glanced down to reread what she'd written. "I'm not even coherent."

She knotted her slender fingers behind her head and slouched back to remember the day before, when the buzzing had begun. She had been coming down the hall from her history final, still wondering whether number five was a trick question, when someone had called her name. The voice had been unmistakable, the careful British inflection that always made her heart pound as if on cue. . . .

"Miss Pennington."

"Yes?" April turned to find Professor Lowry standing in the doorway of his office, his hands on his hips, a perturbed expression on his face.

"Do you type?"

The urgency in his voice caught her off guard, and she had to think about the question. *Do I type? Of course, I type.* "It's my major," she heard herself saying. Then she felt herself blush. "I don't mean typing's my major. I mean my major is business. I wouldn't spend four years here just to learn to type."

She bit her lip and waited, looking past the

professor to the watercolor on his office wall. *Please, God, don't let him think I'm a dodo bird.* She sent up the SOS four times in the endless moment that followed.

Then she heard him laughing a friendly amused laugh that let her know the conversation hadn't ended. "Would you come into my office for just a moment? I have a serious problem."

April stepped across the hall, brushing past Professor Lowry, as he motioned to an overstuffed chair near his desk. His cologne—a clean, crisp fragrance—suddenly made her wonder about her posture.

Straightening her spine, she glanced from left to right. Bookshelves lined the walls—top to bottom—on either side. Behind her next to the doorway were file cabinets, and in front next to a watercolor on the wall was a large window overlooking the front lawn.

"Too bad you can't sit at your desk and look out the window," April said, motioning toward it. "I suppose you need the light coming over your shoulder when you study, but I always like a window to look out of when I'm thinking. Of course, you're so smart you probably don't need to think." She said it guilelessly, as a compliment.

Then she stood next to the overstuffed chair and glanced around the professor's study, looking for things that would tell her more about him. "I'm staring." She smiled at him. "My mother tells me I do that. She says it's bad manners. But I've never been here before. In your office, I mean."

"Won't you sit down?" Professor Lowry motioned toward the chair again and strode over to his desk. April watched him intently as he sat down and leaned back in it. "You're staring again," he said gently.

"Oh!" She quickly searched for something else to look at, found the wastebasket beside his desk, and studied a gold-leaf American eagle.

Professor Lowry followed her gaze to the eagle, watched her carefully for a moment, and then asked hesitantly, "Do you see something I don't?"

"Oh, no!" She put one hand to her lips. "I was just trying not to stare." Then they both laughed, and she remembered why she'd been invited. "You said you had a problem?"

"Yes. I said that, didn't I?" He seemed startled. "I guess you made me forget." He straightened his tie and adjusted his chair.

"I'll go away if that'll help," she offered. "You can call me back when you remember."

"No, that won't be necessary." He frowned slightly. "Unfortunately, it's all coming back to me. At this point, I'd rather have amnesia. You see, I signed a contract to write several chapters for an archaeological textbook. They're due by the end of the school year, and my only free time to work on them is this spring break."

The furrows on his forehead deepened. "Actually, I only have the week before Easter to work on them. The following week, I have a conference in Washington. So you can see my problem."

April nodded seriously. "I can see your problem. In fact, I wouldn't want to wish it on a rattlesnake. But—"

. "You mean you wouldn't want to wish it on a dog, don't you?" Professor Lowry studied her closely. "I believe that's the conventional expression."

She shrugged. "Autumn—my sister—says *rattlesnake*. When you think about it, it makes sense. I mean, dogs are man's best friend, but rattlesnakes are—"

"I see what you mean. Pardon me. I believe I interrupted you again. You said *but*—"

"I don't see how I can help you. You probably don't remember, but I tried archaeology when I first got here. I transferred out after a week."

She lowered her eyes, furiously examining the pink toenails that peeked out of her white sandals. *Now you've done it. You've reminded him what a dummy you are,* she scolded herself.

"Miss Pennington, I don't need help in writing the chapters. I need someone who can type and photocopy, that sort of thing." Professor Lowry broke through her disparagement.

"I can photocopy." She looked up at him eagerly. "I can photocopy just as good as I can type."

"Then you're exactly what I need. My assistant—I should say former assistant—abruptly quit school yesterday." His eyes clouded over, and he was silent for a moment. "She just packed her bags and went home."

He was quiet again, and April, feeling as if he'd forgotten her, cleared her throat.

"If you don't have plans for spring break and would be willing to help me for a week," he went on, "you would be well paid for your efforts." The pleading look on his face softened as she perched in the big chair, ready to jump at a moment's notice. "You would be doing me an immense favor," he added gently. . . .

Suddenly aware of a crick in her neck, April straightened up and looked at her watch. An hour had passed, and she'd barely written her parents a paragraph. Reaching for the clipboard, she tried again to focus her feelings, to translate them into words.

Fifteen minutes later, she admitted defeat, tucked the clipboard under one arm, picked up the backrest, and headed for the women's dorm. It was no use. For the past twenty hours, she'd played the scene in Professor Lowry's office over and over in her head. Now she couldn't stop, not even long enough to write home. Words seemed dull and lifeless compared to the feelings that arose within her when she skipped their conversation and simply let herself remember the emotions.

As she passed Hadley Hall, the double doors opened again, and the salt-and-pepper man reappeared. She smiled happily at him, and he returned the smile, beaming as if the sight of her was good news. April watched him walk to his car, get inside, and drive away.

She knew she was staring, but she didn't care. "Los Lobos, all right. He lives in Los Lobos." She felt certain she was right. "Two kids and a wife. It must be nice to be all settled down, to have your life decided. It must be nice."

Then she let out a whoop for life, tossed a twig at a yellow bird for good measure, and ran up to her empty room. With Soni, her roommate, gone for break, she had their quarters to herself, and she wanted to enjoy every minute.

CHAPTER
TWO

Although Corman Hall housed around 150 women, only 10 of them had remained for the holidays. The telephone in the peach-colored lounge rang repeatedly, its raucous buzz insisting it couldn't be ignored forever. "Hey, Pennington, you got a call." Lola's heavy voice blasted up the stairway.

Girls who referred to each other by their last names irritated April. *You'd think with a name like Lola she'd act more feminine,* April thought as she reluctantly made her way downstairs. She had been cuddled up in Soni's La-Z-Boy thinking of *him*. Nothing Pacific Bell summoned her for could be as interesting.

"The name is April," she called after Lola's disappearing figure as she crossed the foyer to the lounge. "April, like the month."

Lola guffawed. "Sure, Pennington, whatever you say."

The white curtains in the lounge billowed

softly against the windows as April entered. It was a sunny room with a generous fireplace, the furniture grouped invitingly upon the patterned blue carpet. The phone next to the door was off the hook, so she picked up the receiver. "Hello?" She said the word slowly, modulating her voice to disguise her irritation.

"Miss Pennington?" The voice on the line was cordial and decidedly British.

"Professor Lowry?" she replied, fighting against the excitement that raced through her body at the sound of his voice.

"I'm sorry to interrupt whatever you were doing—"

"Oh, I wasn't doing anything. I mean I was breathing and thinking. But I wasn't *doing* anything."

Professor Lowry laughed. "Were you staring?"

"I suppose so." She joined his laughter. "I suppose I always stare when I'm thinking."

"Preferably out a large window."

"Of course, don't you?"

"I don't think, remember? I'm much too smart." His voice teased her.

"Did I say that?" April felt herself blush. She gripped the receiver more tightly, wondering how long she could continue the conversation before her voice betrayed her feelings. "I didn't say that."

"I'm afraid you did."

"Then I apologize. Profoundly and sincerely." She tacked on the adverbs, thinking them urbane and continental.

"It was charming," his tenor voice replied. "I assure you no apology is needed."

There was a momentary lull. And April, determined not to say anything that might be misconstrued, waited for him to continue.

"Now that we've both apologized and both been reassured no apology was necessary, would you join me for Sunday dinner tomorrow at my mother's home? I'm sure we can find more unnecessary things for which to implore each other's forgiveness."

"Sunday dinner?" She intended a gracious acceptance, but all she managed was the half-intelligible phrase.

"I should explain," he added quickly. "My mother isn't well. Since her life is so limited, she takes a great interest in mine. I make a point of introducing my assistants to her as soon as possible."

"Of course, I'll come," April said heartily. "I'd love to meet your mother."

After giving the time, Professor Lowry said good-bye. As he hung up, April clasped the receiver to her heart, cradling it there for a moment before placing it back on the phone.

Then, almost unaware of her movements, she began to waltz about the lounge, the melodies from "My Fair Lady" flooding her imagination as spontaneously as they had followed Liza Doolittle through the movie.

At first she had been disappointed to hear that the invitation wasn't unique, but now she didn't care. Whatever the reason, Professor Lowry was taking her home to meet his moth-

er. "It's a beginning," she whispered triumphantly. "All beginnings have to have a
beginning."

Back in her room, she tried again to write
home. "Professor Lowry just called," she
wrote. "He's taking me home to meet his
mother." The words pleased her, and she
stepped back to study them. Then boldly
scratching out *Professor Lowry*, she penned in
William above it.

" 'William just called,' " she read out loud.
" 'He's taking me home to meet his mother.' "
She giggled. "Much better." She tossed the
clipboard onto the floor and stretched back in
the La-Z-Boy, arching her arms and legs to dis-
tribute her delight evenly about her body.

"William called. William Lowry. Mrs. William Lowry. Mr. and Mrs. William Lowry. April
Lowry. The Lowry children. Aren't they ador-
able? The boy looks just like his father. And the
girl. Well, she's the spitting image of her mother."

An hour later, a knock on the door invaded
April's reverie. After the second knock, Lola
cracked the door open and pushed her head
through. "Hey, Pennington, you alive?"

April turned her head slightly.

"Can I come in?" Lola answered the question herself and came in to sit on the bed oppo-
site the recliner. "Want to have supper?"

April stared past Lola with a puzzled expression on her face.

"You know, supper? It's the third meal of the
day."

April nodded slowly. "Some people call it dinner," she said. "Sometimes it's the second meal."

"Whatever, Einstein. Want to have it? We could walk down to the Macho Taco." Lola stood up, waiting for an answer.

April frowned again.

"I won't call you Pennington for the rest of the evening," Lola offered, sweetening the invitation.

"The rest of spring break and it's a deal." April flipped down the leg rest. "Deal?"

Lola grinned and stuffed her shirt into her jeans. "Don't take away all my fun. The rest of the week—seven days—starting now."

"OK, deal."

The Macho Taco, a college hangout four blocks from campus, specialized in mega-versions of traditional Mexican dishes. As they walked, April remembered she hadn't eaten since breakfast and felt grateful to Lola for pointing her in the direction of food. She had a habit of forgetting to eat and waking up at midnight—ravenous with no place to go.

"It's really strange how Susie Johnson just packed up and left," Lola was saying.

April muttered a nonspecific agreement, more preoccupied with the burrito she planned to have than with her classmate's misfortune, whatever it had been.

"She must have given the dean a reason, but I haven't heard what it was. A good break for you, though. I mean, you getting the job with Lady Killer Lowry and all."

The Macho Taco was still two blocks away. April wished they were already there. "Don't call him that," she said sharply. Then hoping to mask the intensity of her dislike for the nickname, she added, "Why should parents give their children proper names if no one uses them?"

· Lola grinned. "I don't mind using his real name," she said unflappably. "I don't mind calling him Willie. Anyway, it doesn't matter what you call Lowry. Even with no name at all, he's still a looker." And she followed the observation with a long, low wolf whistle.

"Remind me never to go anywhere with you again unless I've got a bag over my head," April whispered severely as an old man in the yard next to them looked up from his gardening.

"Wear your bag next time you come out in public with me," Lola said.

April hadn't planned on bringing it up again, but halfway through her burrito she heard herself asking, "Why do they call him that?"

Lola tapped the bottom of her cup to send the last chunks of ice into her mouth and set it down. "Isn't it obvious *why* they call him *that*? Don't tell me you've never noticed the professor's—how can I put this delicately so it won't offend you—physical attributes?"

"That's not what I mean." April clicked her long nails impatiently. "I mean, when did it start? Who started it?"

Lola shook her head in mock sympathy. "Might have started in his cradle. That man's so gorgeous it might have started in kindergarten."

"Well, it's stupid. And it's dense. It's not even original. Lady Killer. Big deal. Professor Lowry is a very nice person, and I don't think he does anything to merit an ugly nickname like that."

Lola wolfed down a taco in three bites. "Who knows?" she mumbled with a shrug. "People aren't always so obvious, you know. Maybe somebody should ask Susie Johnson."

For the rest of the evening, April felt as if she was running from the words "Maybe somebody should ask Susie Johnson." As hard as she tried to forget them, as hard as she tried not to listen, the words were always there.

After she'd showered, picked out blue ruffled baby dolls, and slipped in between freshly washed sheets, she knew sleep wouldn't come until she allowed herself to ponder Lola's words. As frustrating as Lola's candor could be, she possessed an honesty April respected.

"Lola wouldn't have said that just to be mean," she whispered now as she fluffed the pillows and sat up against them. "It isn't as if I haven't thought it, too. Somewhere deep inside me I can't help thinking that maybe Susie Johnson left because something happened between her and Professor Lowry. And not thinking about it isn't going to do anybody any good."

CHAPTER
THREE

The chirping of birds outside her window woke April the next morning—gently, peacefully. Sometime during the night, she had resolved her dilemma over Susie Johnson's hasty departure. She would get Susie's home phone number from the registrar's office Monday morning and call her. Whatever the truth was she'd face it and deal with it.

Feeling reassured with a plan, she had found herself sinking into the comfort of unremembered dreams, sleep only breaths away.

Now as the world about her slowly focused, she found she'd paid for her nocturnal struggle by oversleeping. Sunday school would begin in fifteen minutes, and she'd be late.

The question then, she thought as she studied herself in the white-and-silver mirror above the vanity table, *is whether to be hurriedly late or leisurely late. Do I take after my father or after my mother?*

Father would dash into his clothes and arrive

huffing and puffing, and slightly grouchy. Mother would take her time and get there when she could, unruffled and smiling, her tardiness smoothed over by her appearance.

As she picked out a blue dress from her closet and a wide ribbon to match, April pondered the fate of children. Through no choice of their own, they were bequeathed portions of their fathers and mothers. "If parents could choose, they'd choose the best of themselves, of course," she said to her image as she sat down to apply her makeup.

What would I give our children? she thought. *William's eyes—so deep brown and caressing. And his chin. My hair.* She took a soft auburn curl and tugged it toward her cheek. *William's intelligence, of course. But my sensitivity. I don't think he feels emotions the way I do.*

The white church was silent as she rounded the corner, stopping to contemplate it from two blocks away. She glanced at her watch. "Half an hour late. Father would have a fit." Quickening her pace, she moved toward the small door on the side that opened into the college-and-career meeting room.

She eased the door shut, then tiptoed over to the back row, and slid into a brown folding chair. *Don't squeak,* she urged it as it began to protest. *I'm barely a hundred and eight pounds on a day when I've eaten. If you think that's bad, I'll have Lola come sit on you. That should make you appreciate me.*

The chair only groaned back, and twenty-three heads turned to look who had just joined them. April smiled weakly, picked up her Bible, leafed through it, and then turned to 1 Corinthians 13 when someone whispered the text in her direction.

Skip Hemmings taught on the love chapter before they broke up into small groups to discuss its practical applications, but although she usually appreciated Skip's insights into the Scriptures, April remained distracted through the rest of the hour. For a reason she didn't understand, she kept thinking about Lola, about what it would be like to be her.

Lola never stood a chance of becoming a cheerleader, being voted homecoming queen, or being wooed as the campus sweetheart. She was tall, awkward, and plain. To say so wasn't even a criticism, it was just a fact.

What puzzled April was that Lola hadn't cultivated the defenses that normally accompanied a body like hers. She didn't make jokes about her looks. She didn't try to camouflage them with clothing or makeup. She didn't stoop. She didn't complain. She didn't apologize.

She was just Lola. Big Lola. Good-humored-about-everyone-and-everything Lola. As April sat in Sunday school and thought about her classmate, she realized she'd never heard Lola talk about her physical appearance, not once in the year they'd lived together in Corman Hall.

The more she thought about it, the more it puzzled her. The more it puzzled her, the more she realized there must be a deeper difference between them than the small irritations that caused her to choose another roommate after their freshman year at King's College.

"April!" Skip Hemmings caught up with her after Sunday school.

April grabbed a doughnut from the coffee table in the church foyer. "Don't say, 'Better late than never.'" She smiled at him.

"'A stitch in time saves nine.'" Skip bounced the old saying back at her with a wave of his big hand.

"'A penny saved is a penny earned.'" She handed him a glazed doughnut.

"Stones gather moss while the road lies vacant."

"That doesn't make sense." She laughed. "How about 'quit while you're ahead!'"

"I would, but unfortunately I'm a body, too." He took her by the elbow and steered her toward the sanctuary. "Wolf that down. There's someone here I want you to meet before the service."

"I don't wolf." She dropped the last half of her doughnut into the trash can and let herself be escorted down the center aisle.

"Peter, I want you to meet someone," Skip called as they neared the third row. A man seated next to a blonde woman in a red dress turned to greet them. In his arms was a small boy of two or three.

"April, this is Peter St. John. Peter, this is April Pennington." Skip motioned toward each as he said their names.

Peter smiled and extended his hand.

"Pleased to meet you," he boomed. "This is David." He bounced the little boy in his arms. "And this is Hannah." The woman next to him stood and extended her hand to April in turn. "And this is Amy." An older girl of four or five popped up into view.

"Pleased to meet you." April returned the greeting pensively. *How did my salt-and-pepper couple from Los Lobos end up here?* she wondered. She surveyed the woman's abdomen carefully. *I was wrong. There isn't another one on the way or, if there is, they've just found out about it.*

She found herself guessing whether they'd driven the station wagon or the Toyota when Peter St. John interrupted her with a question. "I'm sorry," she said hesitantly, unsure of what he'd asked.

"I said you look familiar. Haven't I seen you somewhere?"

His eyes are blue, she thought. *It goes well with salt-and-pepper.* "I have a familiar face," she said sweetly. "I usually remind people of cousins in the country or little sisters back home."

Peter grinned, but shook his head. "No, I've seen you. Recently." He held up his hand in an its-coming-to-me gesture. "The college. The front lawn. I went up to the college yesterday, and you were sitting on the front lawn."

He beamed triumphantly at the woman in the red dress. "There! I knew I'd figure it out." Then he turned back to April. "I remember thinking how much like spring you looked sitting there writing. Yes, you were writing when I saw you.

"And now I find out your name is April. It's perfect!" And he glowed at the group as if he were responsible for how well April's name fit her look.

"Peter's here to talk about a missionary work in Mexico, an orphanage just across the border." Skip broke into the conversation eagerly. "That's why I chose the love chapter to speak on this morning. I'm hoping some of our college-and-career gang will want to be involved." He looked significantly at April.

"I'd certainly like to hear more about it," she said, not sure whether or not she really did, but aware the response was called for. Then the organ began playing, and she found herself being guided into the third row with Peter St. John on her right and Skip Hemmings on her left.

With so many regulars gone for spring break, the church service had an easy, informal feel. Jade Collins, the music director, geared the worship songs to the younger participants, and April happily joined in on the shorter contemporary songs she loved. On either side of her, the men's baritone voices mingled with her soprano, complementing and accenting it.

William has such a beautiful tenor voice, April thought as they paused in the singing to collect the offering. *It's too bad he doesn't attend this church.* Then she imagined him taking the place of either man beside her. Both men were nice enough, but neither compared to William Lowry.

Something had happened to April's thought life in the last twenty-four hours. Although she'd carried William Lowry in her heart since her first week at school, he had always been Professor Lowry. Even in her thoughts. Now some wall had been broken, some barrier crossed. He was William to her, and she knew he'd never be Professor Lowry again.

The worship time ended with prayer, after which Skip Hemmings introduced Peter St. John to the congregation. "He's going to spend five or ten minutes telling about a wonderful missionary work not far from us," he said after Peter had joined him at the podium. "Then after the sermon, he'll be available for individual questions and answers."

"Thank you for inviting me, Skip." Peter shook hands with him and took over the lectern. "I realize many of your regular members aren't here today, but that's OK. Actually, I just need two or three volunteers."

His blue eyes flashed, but then he softened them with a smile. "And I want to say from the beginning," he went on, "that I only want people whom the Lord himself has spoken to. There are a multitude of good works to be done, but they must be done out of obedience and not out of guilt."

April concentrated on his face, wondering what he would look like without the carefully trimmed beard that hid his chinline. Peter went on to tell of a small orphanage in Mexico, how it was caring for over a hundred street children, and how it needed volunteers like himself to translate the gospel into loving arms and smiling faces.

He spoke well, and she found herself caring about the work he was describing more than she'd expected to. There was something contagious about his enthusiasm. As Peter sat down, April looked around and realized others felt it, too.

After the service, Peter and the woman whose name was Hannah, but whom April could only think of as Mrs. Salt-and-Pepper, waited in front of the podium for questions. She thought of joining them, but seeing how many were interested, she waited to catch them on their way out.

Wanting something to pass the time, she began tidying up, walking along the rows and placing the hymnbooks in their racks. She was busy in the last row when someone handed her a hymnbook. Tracking the arm with her eyes, up past a muscled shoulder and strong neck to a graying beard, April realized it was Peter St. John.

"Oh!" She jumped perceptibly and felt herself begin to blush. "I thought you were up in front."

"I was." He stared at her warmly. "But now I'm here."

"And your wife and children?" She searched the room with a sweeping glance.

"Aren't you rushing things?" He continued to stare.

She shoved the hymnbook into its rack, avoiding his stare and hoping to hide her confusion with busywork.

"My sister took her children to the restroom."

April heard the amusement in his voice, glanced up momentarily, and returned to the racks, which were now in perfect order. "Your sister?" She heard her own voice, strained and uneasy.

"Hannah's my sister. Her husband is in the Navy. So when he's away, I help out with the kids."

April knew he was still staring at her. She thought a moment, then grudgingly returned his look. "That makes Amy and David your niece and nephew?"

He nodded.

Her discomfort turned to exasperation. He was enjoying it, and she didn't want him to. "You're the only one I've ever met who stares more than I do," she said accusingly.

"Then we have something in common."

"It's rude, you know."

He nodded again, and his failure to defend himself disarmed her. "Do you own a Toyota?" she asked.

He shook his head.

"Live in Los Lobos?"

"No."

"What do you do for a living?"

"Rushing things again. I'm a junior at UCSB."

April sighed, shrugged, and then laughed a quiet little resigned sound. "I'll have you know you've just shattered my illusions. I saw you at the college, too. And I invented a whole life for you. Now you've gone and crashed it all to pieces."

"My sincere apologies," Peter said teasingly. "But the real me isn't so bad once you get to know me. And I'm not an old man. Just prematurely gray. It happens to some people, you know. I can't help it. It's in my genes."

A shy silence came between them, and they stood quietly as if neither knew how to end the conversation. Finally, he stepped back, extended his hand, and said formally, "It's been a pleasure to meet you."

His handshake was strong and firm. "I enjoyed your talk," she replied. "I'm working at the college the first week of spring break, but I might have some time the second."

"I hope so." He stroked his beard, and she noticed again how blue his eyes were. "The children at the orphanage would love you. Skip has my number. Please call."

"Good-bye." April busied herself with the hymnals, straightening and restraightening them until his footsteps were gone. She hadn't meant to volunteer. Her own words had taken her by surprise. To counter her confusion, she risked a glance about the sanctuary, found it empty, and hurried out a side door toward the comfort of the college campus.

CHAPTER
FOUR

Back at Corman Hall, April changed into an apricot sundress, pinned her hair away from her face in a forties look, and, like a child waiting for the ice-cream man, sat by her window to wait. Professor Lowry appeared promptly at one o'clock.

She watched him from her window, admiring his purposeful walk as he climbed the winding path to Corman Hall. But when he disappeared from view and the buzzer rang in her room, she counted to ten slowly before ringing back to signal she was on her way.

"Never act too eager around a man," she whispered, wondering as she descended the stairs if her mother's dictum was true. "They want to think it's their idea. Eager women scare men off."

She had imagined the scene when their eyes first met. He would be across the foyer by the window, perhaps leaning casually against the long table. His gaze would be riveted on the stairway, thirstily waiting to drink in the sight of her. She would look down demurely as she walked, not lifting her eyes toward him until she reached the bottom of the stairs. Then their glances would meet. . . .

April faithfully kept her part of the scenario, resisting the impulse to look up until she reached the shiny wooden floor. Then, lifting her chin halfway and peering sedately through her lashes, she found he hadn't cooperated.

For a moment, William Lowry was nowhere in sight. Then a scuffling noise caught her attention and she saw his shoes protruding from behind a large green couch. "Professor? Are you all right?" She walked hesitantly across the foyer. "Professor?"

"Miss Pennington?" His voice gave no indication that anything was out of the ordinary. "I'm behind the green couch."

"Yes, I know." She stared down at his meticulously polished shoes. "What I don't know is why."

"I believe you're speaking to my feet," he called. "It would be best if you could come speak to my head."

"Is this better?" She moved to the other end of the couch and kneeled to peer at his wavy brown hair.

"Much." He struggled briefly, twisting his body until he could see her. "I didn't want to scratch the floor, so I just squeezed back here," he said. "This old couch weighs a ton."

"I understand." She waited, a smile playing on her lips.

"Do I look ridiculous?"

"No," she lied politely.

"Yes, I do, but it's worth it."

"OK, you do. What's worth it?" She pushed her face close to the wall. "I don't see anything."

"Just a moment. I believe I've almost dislodged it." More scraping sounds followed, and then Professor Lowry's fist appeared above his head. "Here," he said, dropping something into her hand.

It was a small blue stone. As he pushed himself out from under the couch, April held it up to the light. "It's beautiful," she said. "What kind of stone is it? Do you think it's worth anything? How did it get behind the couch?"

"May I?" He reached for the stone and crossed to the window. "It's a sapphire," he said authoritatively after a moment. "I've learned something about gems. An appraisal will tell how much it's worth. And as to how it became wedged between the floorboards, perhaps only this old couch can tell."

He reached into his suit and slid the stone into his vest pocket. "Shall we go?" he asked with a smile. "My mother has many virtues, but patience is not among them." He bowed slightly, opened the door, and stood aside for her.

"Pardon me for not telling you how lovely you look this afternoon," he said as they reached the parking lot. "Over there." He pointed toward a white Chevy. "I thought it at once, but I was in no position to tell you so."

He laughed. "Perhaps we shall find that our little gem was worth all the trouble."

From her first day on campus, April had been impressed with Professor Lowry's impeccable manners. Unlike other faculty members at King's College—whose human sides were at times painfully obvious—William Lowry seemed to be gifted with an impenetrable chivalry. *He's the most courteous man on earth*, April thought as he opened the passenger door and deftly helped her inside.

They rode in silence as he guided the Chevy around Hadley Hall and down the gravel drive. The wind blew her hair dangerously, and when she reached to close her window, he closed his as well. "You're probably wondering why I was looking under that couch in the first place," he said, glancing at her.

She didn't admit to it, so he continued. "I dabble in more things than I have time for. One is woodworking. The legs of that couch have a peculiar design, and I was studying them when I noticed a sparkle among the floorboards."

Is there anything he doesn't know? April wondered with respect, listening happily to a lecture on woodworking until the white Chevy pulled into a circular driveway leading to a one-story yellow house with white shutters.

Only five miles from the college, the homes in Mrs. Lowry's subdivision had aged well, their wide streets lined with overhanging elms. "They call these Cinderella cottages, don't they?" April asked, noting the scalloped trims.

Professor Lowry nodded. "Mother's dream was to retire in a cottage by the sea. We always let a flat in London. When I moved her here, I couldn't provide the sea so I did my best to find a cottage." He cut the engine. "In a moment, you'll see. It even has a wishing well."

"You're kidding?" April laughed.

"No, I'm serious." He put a finger to his lips. "Wait here. I'm going to bring her out. She'll give you the guided tour. But beware!" His eyes widened. "Of the knickknacks."

Professor Lowry disappeared into the yellow-and-white house, and while April waited, she tried to picture his mother. The house was easy. Even though Mrs. Lowry was English, it would be wall-to-wall early American decor, frilly priscillas, and enough knickknacks to stock a Hallmark store. But when she imagined its owner, all that came to mind was Mother Goose.

The woman who appeared shortly, leaning delicately on her son's arm, was anything but Mother Goose. From her sculptured hair to her fashionable shoes, she could have been a model in *Mature Years*. Equally modern, the interior of her home contained expensive "knickknacks," among them original Hummel figurines that dotted the living room.

This is the woman whose life is so limited? April wondered as she followed Mrs. Lowry's trim figure through the house to the backyard.

"I always begin my tours in the back," Mrs. Lowry said brightly as they stepped onto the

37

patio. "My flower garden is the pride of my life. Other than William, of course." She patted her son's cheek. "Come, I'll introduce you."

The yard was rectangular, a large patch of green bordered by flowers on three sides. A yellow-and-white gazebo adorned the center, with stepping stones leading to it from where they stood. Guarding the gazebo, in front of small white benches, was a red-bricked wishing well.

"You'll recognize the marigolds, of course." Mrs. Lowry led them from left to right around the rectangle. "And the gladiolas." She named each of the twenty-seven varieties proudly, bending occasionally to straighten a petal or pluck a dying leaf.

"They're gorgeous," April said admiringly. "No wonder you're so proud of them. I would be, too. You've captured a little bit of heaven in your backyard, Mrs. Lowry."

"In that case, we'll take tea under the gazebo." Mrs. Lowry beamed her delight. "You'll stay, won't you? I'll have it ready in a moment. William, do see our guest is comfortable." She smiled warmly at April. "I love it so when young people understand."

"Mother, I thought . . . ," William Lowry called as she bustled away, the screen door closing on his words. "I'm sorry," he apologized, turning to April and motioning toward the gazebo. "I'm dreadfully sorry."

"For what?" She watched him curiously. "Your mother is a dear."

"I know. But," he said, lowering his voice heavy with concern, "she's forgotten you were invited for dinner." He shook his head unhappily. "She does this."

"It's OK," April said quickly, eager to reassure him. "I'm not hungry. I don't eat much anyway except for when I've forgotten to eat for a day or two. Then I stuff myself. Don't worry about me. I just ate last night."

They seated themselves in the gazebo, the happy sound of birds chirping about them. "Tea and crumpets are just fine," April added, hoping the term was still used in England.

"You're certain?" He seemed doubtful, but then brightened. "We can dash to a steak house after tea," he said as if the idea amused him. "You may have to drive, though. I'm so hungry I might faint on the way. Unlike you, I'm accustomed to meals at regular intervals."

When the tea service and a platter of scones were arranged neatly on a small table, Mrs. Lowry poured the steaming tea into china cups flowered with forget-me-nots. Then she raised her cup to her lips, breathed its aroma, and set it back on the saucer.

"William shares his young friends with me," she told April. "And it makes me feel young again simply having you around." The older woman talked on about her girlhood, her marriage, and her move to America.

April listened contentedly, sipping tea, nibbling scones, and storing every bit of information that pertained to William. Pausing now and then for polite exclamations of interest from her guests, Mrs. Lowry seemed happy just to reminisce.

When an hour had passed and his mother seemed likely to doze off, William Lowry stood up to kiss her lightly on the forehead. "We'll be leaving now, love," he said gently. "I'll look in on you tomorrow. Shall I take the tea things into the kitchen?"

Mrs. Lowry shook her head. "I'll just sit here for a moment longer. Then I'll do it." She sighed contentedly. "My garden is the most peaceful spot on earth. Thank you for giving it to me, William."

April stood to say good-bye, and Mrs. Lowry turned toward her. "Thank you for sharing tea with me, dear," she said sweetly. "Please come again."

"I will," April replied. "Your garden is lovely and so are you." On impulse, she bent to kiss the older woman. "Thank you for a wonderful time."

As they passed through the living room, Professor Lowry whispered, "Good-bye, mother. Good-bye, knickknacks." He waved whimsically at the figurines. "Take good care of her, lads."

CHAPTER
FIVE

"You worry about her," April said as they stepped out onto the driveway, "about leaving her alone?"

He nodded. "She really should have a chaperone, but she's too stubborn to agree to it."

When they reached the car, she asked solicitously, "How are you holding up? Are you a quivering mass of unfed muscle? Should I drive?"

He laughed. "No, I'm fine." He crossed to the driver's side. "But may I take you to dinner anyway? If you're free, we could drive to Santa Barbara."

He slid behind the wheel, glanced at the clock on the dashboard, and added as if to convince her, "We can discuss the project and call it business. I'll have you back in a couple of hours."

April pressed her lips together, steeling herself against a natural impulse to agree immediately. *Don't let him think you're too eager*, she coached an inner self verging on wild delight. *Let's handle this maturely.*

"Of course, if you already have plans. . . ." His long fingers traced the leather covering on the steering wheel. "I'll understand."

"I had thought of going to the library," she said slowly, thinking it to make it true and then saying it. "But the drive to Santa Barbara is my favorite. And since it's business. . . ." She looked over at him and bit back a smile. "How can I refuse?"

"Santa Barbara it is." He grinned and turned the key, putting the Chevy in reverse. "No other pressing business later this evening?"

"None."

"Then we'll celebrate spring break. I'll have you home by ten, April. May I call you April?"

She nodded, not trusting herself to speak.

"Please call me William." The prospect seemed to please him. "Formalities during the school year are one thing, but since we'll be working together so closely this coming week, it will be a relief to dispense with *mister* and *miss*. We aren't that far apart in age, you know. I'm hardly on my deathbed."

"How old are you?" April asked innocently, her heart pounding rapidly at this sudden turn of events.

"Well." He studied the road ahead seriously. "You're nineteen?"

"Next month."

"Then let's just say I was ancient when you were five—old enough to be your sitter. But by the time you were fifteen, we could have been pals. And by now we would be peers if it weren't for the artificial stratification of college life."

Afraid her voice would tremble when she spoke it, April waited for the darkness of the restaurant to use his given name. Then she used it to ask for the bread basket, tacking it casually at the end of her request. "Would you please pass the bread basket, *William?*"

She imagined them sitting down to a late dinner, the children already tucked in bed, then blushed at her bold imagination. *What would happen if he could read my thoughts?* she asked herself. *I'd probably scare him away forever.*

The twenty-minute drive to Santa Barbara had been pleasant, the blue foaming ocean to one side and the lush countryside to the other. Professor Lowry had talked of his work as they drove, and April had listened more to the sound of his mellow voice than to anything he had said.

The details of archaeology bored her, its precise methodologies and abstract conclusions making her nervous. The popular glamorization of it—Indiana Jones swinging through the jungles in search of golden statues—was more to her liking. Unfortunately, the chapters Professor Lowry was obligated to produce the following week were the boring ones, the glamorous ones left to other persons or other books.

"This is our feast," Professor Lowry said as the waitress exchanged their empty salad plates for steaks. He eyed his large cut lustily. "Feast tonight. Famine tomorrow."

They were silent as he rapidly devoured a third of his steak. Then with a sigh of relief, he put down his fork and looked at her thoughtfully. "I'll apologize in advance," he said.

She looked up questioningly. "For what?"

"For being terrible company this next week."

"Why?"

"I always am when I'm writing. I'll order you about like a caveman with gout, sending you on thankless research missions and boring you with the most tedious portions of my work. I'll be holed up in a corner, working day and night, metamorphosing from Dr. Jekyl to Mr. Hyde in a deterioration of mind and body unfit for civilized observation."

He shuddered and she giggled. "I'm serious, sweet April." He set down his water glass, drops of moisture still glistening on his lips. "We're embarking upon a grueling journey." He held her eyes with his, and she felt her face flame at the intimacy of the moment.

Unsure how to steady her jangled nerves, April searched for a witty comeback. "Don't worry about me," she said lightly. "I'm from simple peasant stock. We have an astonishing capacity to endure."

This response pleased him, and he laughed unguardedly, the tension of the moment fading as she joined him. But the words he'd spoken hovered with her in that small space between the heart and the breastbone where emotions are felt as physical realities. *Sweet April. I'm serious, sweet April.*

It was still day when they left the restaurant. April found herself surprised at the light outside. In her mind, it had been evening, the dinner only a prelude to a moonlit walk in the sand.

"We have the whole evening left," Professor Lowry said, smiling down at her. "Your wish is my command."

"I'd love to walk on the beach," she said hesitantly.

"As would I." The suggestion seemed to please him immensely. "You're dressed so beautifully I thought you might object to the sand."

"This?" She looked down at her sundress and sandals. "Never. I'm always dressed for the beach. Or at least, I can get that way. Just park and leave me in the car for a minute to take off my stockings. . . ."

There are days when Santa Barbara appears indistinguishable from a postcard. As they traveled past the waterfront parks, April imagined their surroundings in stop-action freeze framing. The tatooed teenager with the long braids fixed in her mind—his lanky frame posed against the horizon to toss a Frisbee to his golden retriever. She imagined herself writing home on the back of the card:

This is what it looked like on the water-front as William and I drove to the beach. I wish you could meet him, Mom and Dad.

*He's more wonderful than I thought. I can't
wait for you to come back from Europe so
you can get acquainted.*

At the southern end of the waterfront, Professor Lowry pulled the Chevy into a parking space, turned off the engine, removed his jacket, shoes, and socks, then handed April the key. "I'll wait for you over there," he said, pointing to a tall palm fifty feet away.

Quickly slipping off her sandals, she wiggled out of her stockings, locked the car, and ran to join him. He had unbuttoned his shirt, stuffed his tie into his pocket, rolled up his shirt sleeves and pant legs. He was leaning back against the palm, pensively contemplating the scenery, when she reached him.

For a moment, she imagined them as actors in a vitamin commercial. *Life is so good,* a husky voice-over proclaimed to the music of violins. *Live it to the fullest. Take vitaminasolatabs. The only ones with a complete daily supply of all the vitamins in the alphabet, especially LMNOP and XYZ.*

Laughing silently at her twists of imagination, she stood beside him, waiting to be acknowledged. Finally, he looked down at her and said, "I was thinking of my mother. In all the changes of my life, she's been the constant factor. Now I wonder if I'm wise enough to care for her when she needs me most."

As they walked toward the water, Professor Lowry explained that his mother was suffering from hardening of the arteries. "Can't something be done?" April asked. "Some medication or something?" She thought of her own parents, so fit and healthy although so far away, and wondered how she would feel if it were her mother.

William Lowry shook his head, "Not at her age," he said sadly. "She told you I'm an only child. What she didn't tell you was that she had eleven miscarriages before me. She was almost forty when I was born.

"I've offered to leave my apartment and come live with her," he said as they sat on the dry sand, stretching their legs to meet the tide. "But she won't hear of it. She's incredibly proud, and I won't rob her of that. I won't submit her to the indignities we heap on our elderly in the name of love."

As the sun met the ocean, blazing the sky above with its setting colors, Professor Lowry added to his mother's story, lingering on his happy preschool days at home and the fulfilling college years at Oxford. April, content again merely to listen, sat beside him, warming her soul in his words.

Then as a chill blew up from the ocean breeze, she began to shiver. Taking note of this, he stood to extend a hand. "You're a good listener, April Pennington," he said as he pulled her to her feet. "I don't know when I've talked so much about myself to one person."

"You're an interesting talker, William Lowry," she replied. Then bolting ahead, she yelled playfully, "Race you to the car. Last one there's a rubber chicken."

He accepted her challenge easily, waiting nonchalantly on the hood of his car as she panted up to it. "What next, rubber chicken? Home, window shopping, or the movies?"

"The movies!" April clapped delightedly. "They're having a Bogie festival in town. I saw it in the paper. Maybe we won't be too late if we hurry."

He whipped open her door, raced around to the other side, hopped in, and gunned the engine. "Here's looking at you, kid," he said in a miserable imitation of Humphrey Bogart. Upon reaching the theater only fifteen minutes late, they bought popcorn and sneaked down the darkened aisle to the front of the theatre. The movie was *The Treasure of the Sierra Madre*. April settled back to enjoy its familiar scenes on the screen and Professor Lowry's unfamiliar presence by her side. *A perfect ending to a perfect day*, she thought happily as she dipped into the buttered popcorn.

Hot fudge sundaes at an old-fashioned ice-cream parlor completed the day, and the two arrived back on campus just short of ten. "Thank you for a wonderful time," he said as they parted on the steps of Corman Hall. "What a pleasant way to start off the week."

"Thank you," she said demurely. "I had a wonderful time, too."

Then William Lowry was gone, his muscular frame bounding off with schoolboy enthusiasm. "It's been the most wonderful evening of my life," April whispered to the stars as she paused to search for a familiar constellation.

Finding none, she chose a bright, sparkling star over Hadley Hall and wished on it. "Starlight, star bright, brightest star I've seen tonight. Wish I may, wish I might, have the wish I wish tonight."

She took a deep breath, then spoke her wish softly, the moon and the trees and the stone steps her only witnesses. "I wish all our weeks would begin so beautifully and stay beautiful the other six days as well."

Inside the foyer, April found a note with her name on it pinned to the bulletin board. Opening it absentmindedly, she was annoyed to find it was from Peter St. John. "Please call me in the morning," the note said, giving his telephone number. "It's urgent."

April folded and refolded the white paper as she climbed the stairs. *What could be so urgent?* she thought irritably. *And why did he come all the way over here? It isn't as if we really know each other.*

Part of her knew this reaction to Peter's note was irrational, his request certainly not a heinous crime. But she hadn't wanted to think of anything except William. She had wanted to float up the stairs in sublime solitude and drift off to sleep surrounded by the memory of him alone.

Now, she was thinking of Peter St. John instead. And wondering what could be so urgent. And feeling angry with him for coming to Corman Hall. And resenting that she had to call him in the morning before she saw William again. And resenting that she was resenting something when she only wanted to be savoring the ecstasy of her evening.

Her dreams that night further fueled her resentment toward Peter St. John. Instead of dreaming of William, she dreamed of Peter and Mexico and hundreds of sniffling orphans. Then, unable to sleep past six-thirty, she showered, read a meditation for the day, and went to the lounge to call Peter.

"This is April Pennington," she said tersely when he answered. "You left a note for me to call."

"April!" He seemed overjoyed to hear her voice.

"You said it was urgent."

"Yes, it is. Absolutely urgent. I'm so glad you called. I must see you right away. Where can we meet?"

CHAPTER
SIX

It had rained during the night. The early morning sky was gray and cold as April sped across the front lawn, the wet grass slippery beneath her feet. March could never be counted on, sunny one day, like this the next.

Peter had trapped her into breakfast. "I'm glad you called before breakfast," he'd said without asking if it was true. Before she could answer that she didn't eat breakfast, he had continued with, "Let's meet at The Nook in twenty minutes."

She was hurrying now to meet him—with barely enough time to slip on jeans and put on makeup—when she should be dressing for William. "This had better be important," she murmured, smoothing down the collar of her turtleneck sweater. "I'll only stay long enough to find out. Maybe have a cup of coffee."

The Nook, usually overrun by college students escaping Campus Food Service, seemed small and lonely as she approached the corner of Main and Orchard. Glancing about in all four directions, April realized she was the only person in sight. It seemed unnatural, and she wondered if weekday mornings were always this desolate when the college emptied out for holidays.

Peter was waiting for her. He had said twenty minutes and she'd taken thirty. She had imagined him behind a rancher's breakfast—steak, eggs, potatoes, flapjacks, honey biscuits, freshly squeezed orange juice, and coffee so thick it poured like gravy. Instead, he was reading the paper, the tabletop in front of him empty.

"I'm over here!" He stood up and waved to her as she opened the door. It seemed so incongruous that she smiled in spite of herself. The diner was empty except for two grandmotherly types in the corner and a small man at the bar. Even if it had been full, she could have located him in a glance.

"I came as soon as I could," she said as she slid into the booth. It sounded as if she cared that she'd kept him waiting, so she added, "I can't stay long. I'm working on campus this week, you know."

He nodded. "It won't take long. I just need the female perspective on something."

"Couldn't you ask Hannah?" April didn't bother hiding the irritation in her voice. It was bad enough to be rushed out into the cold world on truly important business. She had expected him to personalize his Sunday morning plea, motivated perhaps by some unfortunate turn of events.

There was a message waiting for me at home yesterday, he would say. *Half the staff has pneumonia and the children need nursing as well. I'm leaving this afternoon. We don't know each other well, but I saw the compassion in your eyes as I spoke about the orphanage and I thought. . . .*

She had rehearsed her response.

I'm glad you sensed that, she would say, *because I do care.* She would pause a moment to gaze pensively out the window. *If only I hadn't already committed myself to such an important project. Professor Lowry was left without help at the last moment, and he's needed in Washington next week. I'm terribly sorry, but you'll have to find someone else. . . .*

But Peter St. John's "urgent" business obviously wasn't urgent at all. His sister, Hannah, could give him the "female perspective." Or his mother. Or his next-door neighbor. Or his girl friend.

"I need an impartial opinion," Peter said calmly. "Hannah just laughs and tells me they all look cute." He poked his index finger into his right cheek. "I don't want to look cute." The waitress came to take their orders before he could explain.

"Just coffee," April said.

"The same." Peter smiled charmingly.

She frowned. "Don't you eat breakfast?"

"Never."

"Then why are we here?"

"So you can tell me what to wear." He spread his hands out as if to say, "Isn't it obvious? Where else would we meet to discuss this?"

"You had to see me *right away, absolutely urgent* to ask me what to wear?"

"Not what to wear actually. Which to wear. Here. I'll show you." He reached down and pulled up a large briefcase. "And it is urgent," he said as he set the case on the tabletop. "I have to pick her up this afternoon."

"Her?"

"Karen. She's a nurse. It's a blind date. I've never seen her before." He began taking bow ties from the case and lining them up in front of April. "Let's start with the ties. I don't want to make a mistake."

They were large ties—three or four times the size of a normal bow tie—and all April could think as she looked at them was that they must have been used in a Marx Brothers movie. One was bright red with yellow chickens on it. Another was forest green with purple stars. A third had orange and white clowns on a shocking pink background.

Struggling to control the amusement that now replaced her irritation, she asked, "What effect are you looking for?" The waitress arrived with the coffee, and April busied herself with the cream and sugar to keep from laughing.

Peter tugged at his beard pensively. "Normal, I guess. And younger. I want to look my age."

"Are you old?" She blew across her coffee, thinking it would be physically impossible to blow and laugh at the same time. He had to be joking, but she wasn't absolutely sure.

"Just twenty-one. I'm not *old*." He said the word carefully, as if it would break if he misused it. "Honest. So which one should I wear? I thought you would know."

April decided to play his game. It was too much fun not to. She'd be furious with him afterwards when he admitted it was all a joke, then tell him he had no right to spoil her morning with such foolishness. "This one." She picked out the red bow tie with the yellow chickens.

"You're right." He nodded enthusiastically. "I would have come to the same conclusion myself. You're absolutely right. Now the glasses." He put away the bow ties and pulled out four pairs of heavy horn-rimmed glasses. Only the shape of the lenses differed.

"Do you usually wear glasses?" she asked, wondering if he was wearing contacts.

"No. Just to dress up. To look younger, you know. They're not prescription."

"Then wear this one." She picked out the worst of the lot, wide rectangular ones. "What else? You'll wear your hair parted down the middle, of course."

"Should I? Do you think it'll stay?" He made a part with his fingers and pushed at his thick hair.

"Use mousse." She stirred her coffee vigorously.

"I never would have thought of it."

"Buy some. What else?"

"Well, I have saddle shoes."

"Of course. Brown and white?"

"No, green and white." For a moment, he looked worried. "That won't be too much, will it? I have green pants and my high school letterman's sweater."

"No, it'll be perfect. Just don't forget the mousse. You'll ruin the whole effect if you leave it the way it is. But the bow tie will be stunning with the green."

"Great." He stored the glasses back in the briefcase, clicked it shut, and set it back down on the floor. "I'm so relieved." He reached for his coffee and mixed in three creams. "Thank you so much for coming."

"You're welcome." She stood up to leave. He hadn't given her any reason to believe it was all a joke—except for the fact the whole thing was completely ridiculous. So she decided to keep playing it straight. "I'm glad I could help, but I have to be going now."

He stood up to watch her leave. "I won't forget the mousse," he called as she opened the door. "I'll stop at Thrifty on the way home."

"Good." She made an OK sign with her thumb and forefinger before she turned down Main Street toward the college. Then as an afterthought, she walked back to The Nook, stuck her head in the door, and called softly, "You can come by the dorm later this evening if you want to tell someone how it went."

"Thanks. If I'm not too late." He waved

good-bye again, and April thought what a happy person he seemed to be.

Sort of twinkly. It's his eyes, she told herself, thinking of their deep blue color and the way little lights shone in them when he spoke. *He has nice eyes, but there's no way of knowing if he's really handsome. Beards can hide so much.*

She had made a vow never to date a beard. Not seriously, anyway. She had learned her lesson with Frank Wetzel. He'd transferred to Oakton High in his senior year, his reputation as a heartthrob preceding him because Susie McVie was friends with his cousin. "I met him this summer and he's an absolute doll!" She had swooned around school the week before Frank's arrival.

April had hoped Susie was right. She had just broken up with Travis Johnson, captain of the football team/top of the heap, and anyone else on campus would have been a step down unless Frank lived up to his reputation. He was coming complete with honor roll and basketball credentials, and might be perfect to finish out the year.

April and Frank were going steady in less than a week—the solution to each other's dilemma in a world where status was king—and life was perfect until the accident. They were coming home from a party when a drunken driver rammed Frank's Trans Am, sending it spinning out of control until it landed in a drainage ditch.

Lots of things were broken, the drunken

driver killed—which was unusual, April's mother said, because they hardly ever got what they deserved—and the last half of their senior year hopelessly spoiled. But the shocker had come for April when she saw Frank's face without his beard.

The nurses had shaved it off to stitch a long gash in his cheek. And when April saw him for the first time, she didn't recognize him because he had no chin. Without the beard, his face was as round as a melon, the point where his chin should be barely visible at all.

The experience of learning that Frank Wetzel had no chin had remained with April as a metaphor for life. On graduation day, she realized she was through with jocks and beards, vowing to look for more substantial and trustworthy men.

After a week on campus at King's College, she had realized the sum of all substantial and trustworthy men could be found in the person of Professor William R. Lowry. Clean-shaven, dignified, dedicated, and strikingly handsome, Professor Lowry embodied everything she wanted in a man. This had left her free to date for fun—beards or no beards—because her heart belonged to the assistant professor of the archaeology department.

CHAPTER
SEVEN

It began to drizzle as April walked back toward the campus. She had counted on arriving in time to change before joining William Lowry in his office. But the nonsense with Peter had taken longer than she'd planned, and now she had to choose between going as she was or going late.

Neither option conformed to her mental image. She had carefully selected her clothes the night before—a cream linen suit with a ruffly blue blouse and one-inch heels to match—to give the impression of junior executive. Junior executives were never late unless they could claim "pressing business in another part of town."

"I'd better go as is," she decided, casting around for another way to feel about rushing into Professor Lowry's office, looking like a schoolgirl. It quickly came to her as a music video. The music itself wasn't important, something old-fashioned and nostalgic. It was the picture that mattered.

The day was perfect, gray and rainy, enveloping everyone in its doldrums except for one lighthearted girl. . . .

Enter lighthearted girl. Walking. No, almost floating up the front lawn to an ivy-covered building where the tragic figure of a handsome, but moody, professor huddles—pressed about, downtrodden—by the grayness.

Follow lighthearted girl as she enters the ivy-covered building. Notice how the radiance of her being—characterized by the casualness of her dress (light brown sweater and blue jeans) and the windsweptness of her hairstyle (sprinkled with raindrops that seem to glow)—lights up the dreary halls.

Pan to the professor's face as the lighthearted girl enters his office. . . .

By the time April reached Professor Lowry's office, she had convinced herself that gracious and natural was the best way to appear. "I don't want him to think I'm trying too hard to impress him," she told herself as she rounded the stairs to the second floor. "The linen suit would have been too dressy."

Unfortunately, she could have been wearing a potato sack. Professor Lowry hadn't been joking about the nastiness that overtook him when he was writing. For one thing, she had never seen him at work in rolled-up shirt sleeves.

But there he was—scrunched up at his type-writer—with both sleeves unevenly rolled. He looked as if he'd been there for hours. She didn't ask. Instead, she just stood in the doorway, timidly waiting for an invitation to enter. The room looked as rumpled as its owner.

His coat and tie were thrown across the overstuffed chair in a fashion sure to wrinkle them. Textbooks had been opened and left in untidy heaps, and crumpled wads of typing paper were strewn about the floor. Worst of all, the shade was drawn across the window, making the day seem even more dreary.

When it became apparent that he wouldn't notice her unless she announced herself, April reached down to pick up some of the paper wads near the open door. She had three in her hand when a voice stopped her.

"Don't," Professor Lowry barked over the clack of the typewriter keys. "It'll just get worse."

She told herself later that it only sounded like a bark because of the typewriter in the background, but momentarily, she felt rebuked. *Of course, it'll get worse if you never pick it up*, she thought without saying so. She stood at attention again, the papers falling from her opened fist.

The typewriter clacked on, and when she realized she wanted to bite a nail, she dared to speak. "What should I—"

"I've written out your instructions for the day. You won't have trouble following them. I've called UCSB library. They know you're coming. Everything you need is on top of the filing cabinets. Call if you have any questions."

April glanced at the filing cabinets. A small cardboard box had her name on it. Taking the box, she stood wondering how she was supposed to reach the university. "How should I—"

"Use my car. The keys are in the box."

So they were. She would have seen them if she'd bothered to look. Not knowing whether to thank him or say good-bye or wish him a profitable day, she hesitated, said nothing, and left feeling like Dorothy after her first visit with Oz, the Great and Wonderful.

Professor Lowry's car was parked in front of Hadley Hall. She put the box down on the hood, then checked through it carefully. Her day's work would consist of researching specific questions—mechanical and boring. Thankful for the drive to put things in perspective, she placed the box on the front seat, slid in behind the wheel, and started the engine.

"It isn't as if he didn't warn me," she told herself as she sped onto the freeway. "He even apologized in advance." It helped to think of the morning's complexity in this way. "It's just that I've never seen this side of Professor Lowry before."

The person she'd met this morning wasn't *William* to her—at least not yet. *William* was always neat and charming and breathtaking. It would take awhile to incorporate his alter ego into her image of him. "Of course, I should have known he would have a dark side," she reassured herself. "All brilliant people do."

The sun was coming out over the ocean, but

April scarcely noticed it. All the way to the university, she struggled between two voices. The loudest told her that she must have sensed he was moody, that it was part of his allure, that his loftiness attracted her. The other voice—weak and hidden because she worked against it—told her it was no different from Frank Wetzel's lack of a chin.

The head librarian, a round wispy-haired woman with a collage of grandchildren pictures on her wall, greeted April kindly. "Don't hesitate to ask if you have a problem," she told her. "Professor Lowry is a favorite here."

You mean William, April thought. *I'm sure you've met William, not Professor Lowry.* She was already thinking of him as some sort of Transylvanian prince who dared show his dark side only to his most trusted advisers.

The work was tedious, but uncomplicated. She was looking mainly for quotes and sources, which she listed on the yellow pads below each of Professor Lowry's queries. When the quote was too long to write out, she stood in line to use a copy machine. Halfway through the day, she remembered her resolution to call Susie Johnson.

Susie, a senior majoring in archaeology, had been Professor Lowry's assistant for three years. April knew she lived in Colorado, somewhere near Denver, and that she came from a large family. She didn't know her well enough to call and simply say hello.

I'll call and tell her I'm working for Professor Lowry. Maybe she'll volunteer some informa-

tion, April thought doubtfully as she dialed the registrar's office to ask for Susie's number. She had tried to befriend Susie as a way of getting closer to William, but Susie had been cool to her in the way upperclassmen often were.

Luckily, Mrs. Halfmeyer answered the phone, recognized April's voice, and didn't question her request. "Tell Susie we miss her," Mrs. Halfmeyer said before she hung up. "Tell her we hope she'll be back after the holidays."

"Thank you," April said. Mrs. Halfmeyer had given her the perfect excuse. She'd simply call Susie and ask if she was coming back to campus. She'd explain she was working for Professor Lowry over spring break and wanted to continue as his assistant if Susie wasn't returning.

It's a little cold, but I'll be nice about it, April thought as she went to the librarian to exchange a five-dollar bill for quarters. *I can't think of any other good reason to call, and I can't out-and-out ask her if she left because something was going on between her and William.*

It felt odd to be dialing long distance from a public telephone in the middle of the day. Her mother had taught her to be thrifty with phone calls, and she felt un-American as she poked quarters into the slot at the operator's instructions. Susie's mother answered on the third ring.

"This is April Pennington calling from King's College," April said formally. "May I please speak to Susie?"

"Of course," Mrs. Johnson said. "Just a moment."

Susie was either far away or reluctant to come to the telephone because the minutes ticked by and the operator asked for more quarters before April heard Susie's voice on the line. "April?" She sounded tired.

"I'm sorry. Did I wake you?" April tapped her heel nervously against the green tile.

"No, I was just resting."

Silence.

"Did you want something, April? You called."

Say something bright and cheerful, April. "Mrs. Halfmeyer says to tell you everyone misses you." *Everyone is probably overdoing it.* She wants to know if you'll be back this year." *Then why didn't Mrs. Halfmeyer call herself?* "Actually, that's why I called. I'm filling in for you with Professor Lowry over spring break. I'm enjoying the work, but I don't know if you'll want it back when you—"

"Tell Mrs. Halfmeyer I'm not coming back. Not this year anyway. Tell her I'll write the Dean of Women to formally withdraw from school."

Silence.

"Susie, what happened?" April blurted out in a rush of sympathy. "You sound so . . . so tired."

"I am. And morning sick. All the time." Susie laughed weakly. "April, I'm pregnant. But don't worry. We've decided to get married. He's flying out to meet my family next week.

The news will be all over campus when he gets back. We've decided not to hang our heads in shame. It's the eighties. These things happen."

Thunderstruck silence.

"April?"

"I–I thought–I thought he was flying to Washington." April's voice trembled.

"Washington? Whatever gave you that idea?"

"That's what he told me. He said he only had this week to work on the book because he had to be in Washington for a conference."

"Who are we talking about?"

April cleared her throat and barely whispered into the receiver, "Professor Lowry?"

"Professor Lowry?" For a moment, Susie must have forgotten she was morning sick because she roared with laughter. "You thought I was talking about the professor? Don't be silly! That's impossible. I'm talking about Paul Crypher, of course. We've decided to get legal."

April began to breathe again, the air sweet to her lungs. "Congratulations, Susie! I'm so happy for you. Paul's a great guy. I didn't know you were going together."

Susie gave a short, dry laugh that seemed to catch in her throat. "Thanks," she said. "You're not the only one. Tell the professor I'll be calling him. And the job is yours if he offers it to you."

CHAPTER
EIGHT

It took April several minutes to stop quivering. She felt as if she'd just come off a roller-coaster ride. *You thought I was talking about the professor? Don't be silly! That's impossible.* Susie's words echoed reassuringly through her mind as she finished her work at the library and headed back toward King's College. *Impossible, of course. Lola was way off. William wasn't that type of person.*

Another of Susie's responses was less reassuring. "The job is yours if he offers it to you," she had said. *If he offers it to you.* April had mistakenly assumed the job was hers if Susie didn't return. The truth was that Professor Lowry hadn't offered her a permanent position. Not yet.

"Well, he won't find fault with my work," she told herself, giving the box next to her a proud little pat. She had completed all his queries in neat, precise penmanship or clear, clean photocopies, and she hadn't called once for clarification. She had understood his instructions perfectly.

"Susie left because of Paul Crypher," she told herself, a smile breaking out on muscles that had been tensed all day. "Nothing was going on between her and William.

"Lady Killer Lowry is just an unfortunate nickname. And I'm going to do such a good job that he'll hire me until I graduate." At the moment, that seemed like an eternity.

Professor Lowry's office was dark and silent when she reached it. Flipping on the overhead light, she found a note with her name on it taped to a file cabinet: "Gone to check on Mother. Leave the info on the cabinet. I'll have a new batch for you in the morning."

It wasn't signed. "At least he remembers his mother, no matter what," she said as she studied the room. His coat and tie were gone. She assumed he'd tidied up a bit before going to visit the white-and-yellow house. "A dutiful son makes a dutiful husband." It sounded like a wise old saying, but she wondered if she'd made it up to suit the moment.

Her first impulse was to clean up the office. Her second impulse was to think that Professor Lowry wouldn't appreciate it. "There must be a good way to think about this," she told herself as she turned out the light and closed the door, leaving it ajar as it had been when she arrived. "If only I can figure out what it is."

When she reached the dorm, Lola invited her out for dinner again. "We can go for

Chinee foo this time," she said, pulling her eyes into slits with her thumbs.

"Next time," April said, heading for the stairs. "Thanks."

"Did you eat today?" Lola asked suspiciously.

"Breakfast." April turned around.

"What did you have?"

April mumbled the truth. "Coffee."

"Whew! That's a relief." Lola wiped her brow in an exaggerated motion. "For a moment there, I thought you might be going anorexic on us."

April laughed. "Next time, really," she said as she climbed the stairs. "Right now I just want to soak in a hot bath."

There was only one tub to four showers on April's wing, but since she was alone for the holidays, no one would fight her for it. "I'll use bath crystals and soak until I get pruney," she murmured as she wrapped herself in Soni's big blue towel and headed down the hall.

It took several minutes in the fragrant, steamy water before she lost the sense of its being a mortal sin and gave in to the luxury of "hogging the tub." It was long and pink, and she could bury herself in it from chin to toe without spilling water into the overflow. *I'm going to have a big tub like this in my home*, she thought lazily.

Her ears were under the water when a knocking in the background brought her to the surface. "April, are you in there?" It was Lola.

"Yeah. Use the tub on your own floor."

"Penning—April, you have a visitor."

"Who?" April sat upright in the tub, sloshing water into the overflow.

"A man."

"Who?" April covered herself with her arms. *Maybe William's here to apologize for treating me like a slave.*

"He says his name is Peter St. John." Lola jiggled the doorknob. "He's real cute. I'll take him if you don't want him."

"Peter St. John." She'd forgotten he might be coming. "You make him sound like a puppy dog, Lola. Tell him I'll be five minutes." Then she thought of something funny and smiled to herself. "You know they don't allow pets in the dorm."

"I could keep him in the closet and only let him out at midnight." Lola guffawed and left, her shoes clumping unevenly against the rest-room tile.

Five minutes was impossibly short for meeting a man. April's mother had taught her to always put her best face forward. That took at least twenty minutes for the face alone. "But since he insists on being so unorthodox, he'll get a two-minute face," April decided as she dried herself in front of the full-length mirror.

"In fact, I'll give him a zero-minute face!" She bent over, put a small towel to the base of her neck, and wrapped her hair in it. Then she wrapped her body in the blue towel, collected her things, and ran to her room.

From the time she was seven, she had dressed to meet a man of any sort. Even her father. At first, she hadn't understood—coming to the breakfast table on her seventh birthday in her bathrobe and being told to change immediately—why one day could make such a difference. Then her mother began to teach her what it meant to be a lady, and it had everything to do with looking perfect, if possible. . . .

"Of course, there are times when you just can't," her mother had said sensibly. "But try to save those times for the girls. That's why I'm against all this new stuff about the father being in the delivery room. Men and women weren't meant to mix at a time like that. . . ."

Now the old rebellion—buried by the age of ten—arose from some place she wasn't aware of. She would put on a flannel nightgown, slip into her velveteen robe, and go to meet Peter with her hair wrapped in a towel. The thought of it brought a flush to her cheeks and a dizzy feeling to her head.

Lola and Peter were on the couch, animatedly discussing the Lakers, when April stepped into the foyer. Her slippered feet had been silent on the staircase, and her appearance was unannounced.

"Pennington!" Lola's voice carried the rebuke April would have expected from her mother.

"You promised not to call me that," April said with a laugh. "I see you've gotten acquainted."

Lola blushed—something April had never seen her do before.

Peter stood up, smiling at April. "I have season tickets at the forum. Lola's going with me on Friday." His glasses were off, but he put them back on for effect. He was dressed exactly as they had agreed that morning.

"So let me have a look at you," April said, thinking, *Why are you always telling me about other women?* "Turn around." She motioned for him to model his outfit. "You look wonderful!" she said, bursting into a cackle that sounded like Lola's. Peter looked like a total nerd, from his plastered hair to his green-and-white shoes.

"Thank you." His face reddened slightly. "I think the hair does it, don't you? The mousse wasn't enough. I had to add a little Vaseline."

"Well, next time you'll know." April cleared her throat. "Did your blind date like it? The whole effect, I mean."

"She was overwhelmed." Peter nodded thoughtfully. "We won."

"Won?" April felt suddenly maternal. Her pupil had won something. "Won what?"

"The contest." Peter straightened his bow tie and posed again. "Karen was the perfect counterpart."

"For what?" Lola asked.

There has to be a joke here somewhere, April thought.

"I guess April didn't tell you," Peter said. "I had a blind date tonight with a girl named Karen. She's a nurse. Very nice, but a little medical. She kept identifying the chicken parts by their biological names.

"Anyway, we went to a Nerd Party. And we

won!" He stepped forward for congratulations. "Don't be shy. Applause is appreciated. Money is preferred."

"April didn't tell Lola because Peter didn't tell April," April said severely.

"Didn't I?" Peter's face was a mask of remorse, except for his eyes, which twinkled suspiciously. "You must have wondered! Why didn't you say something?"

"I've been taught not to be rude," she said severely again, but then he struck her as so silly looking that she laughed. "It's OK. I forgive you. And you look marvelous."

The towel around her head was slipping, and she stopped to adjust it. "As you can see, I'm on my way to bed. Lola's wonderful company. You two probably have more than just the Lakers in common."

"I'm sure we do." Peter looked at Lola warmly, and April thought she blushed again. "Don't worry about me."

What made you think I would? April thought. "Good night," she said politely. "Congratulations, again."

By the time she reached the stairs, Peter and Lola were back on the couch, laughing and carrying on as if she didn't exist. "Don't worry about me," April whispered to the flowered wallpaper, and in her mind, she heard Peter St. John answer back, "What made you think I would?"

CHAPTER
NINE

April was near the window, staring out at the night shadows, the room dark around her when Lola tapped softly on the door. For a moment, April didn't answer, debating whether to pretend she was asleep. Then she called, "Come in."

Lola opened the door quietly, shut it behind her, and sat down on the La-Z-Boy. For a long time neither of them spoke, the ticking of the Swiss clock on the wall the only accompaniment to their breathing. Finally, Lola said, "Doesn't that clock drive you crazy?"

"I'm used to it." April reached out to touch the windowpane. It was cold and hard. "My folks sent it to me from Switzerland. It gives me a cozy feeling."

"So how come you went down to meet Peter in your bathrobe?"

"What was worse? The bathrobe or the towel around my hair?"

"All of it. So how come? It's not like you."

April thought of a flip answer, but checked it at the mixture of anger and concern in Lola's voice. Finally, she said simply, "Am I so *predictable?*"

"I didn't mean it that way." Lola came to sit on the bed next to her. "But I know you pretty well."

The moon came out from behind a cloud, lighting the night outside the window and shining into the room. April turned to look at her friend. "Professor Lowry sat in a darkened office, typing away in his shirt sleeves all day. His office was a mess," she said as if it explained something.

Lola smiled slightly. "So that's why you went to see Peter in your bathrobe?"

"No!" April shook her head. "Yes. Maybe. The point is that it's hard to really *know* anybody. I mean, who would have thought that Professor Lowry would go caveman when he writes? Anyway, why does it bother you how I meet Peter St. John?"

It was Lola's turn to be silent.

The Swiss clock ticked away the minutes in the background. Then April said, "Tell me, Lola. I've been thinking about how you and I don't share inside things. Tell me, even if you think I won't approve."

"I'm the one who doesn't approve," Lola said slowly.

When she didn't explain, April asked, "Of what?"

"Of the reason why I felt angry with you for coming down to meet Peter in your bathrobe."

Lola sighed and moved back to the La-Z-Boy. "I don't like it when I judge people by how they look."

April waited.

"When the buzzer rang and I opened the door, I took to Peter right away because he looked so outrageous." Lola chuckled. "I guess that's a looks judgment, too, but it's all right.

"When you came down in your bathrobe, I assumed you were doing it to spite him. I have this image of *girls like you* putting down nice guys like Peter just to prove they're hot stuff. Sort of for sport. But I don't feel right when I judge people that way."

"*Girls like me?*" April deliberately copied Lola's intonation. She felt sorry they'd opened up "inside things," but there was nothing to be done about it now. It had been such a strange day, and if she could choose, she'd end it now, hoping for a better one tomorrow.

"Did I say it that way?" Lola came back to the bed. "It's unfair of me, April. You're so cute and pretty. Sometimes I think you're a snob." Then she added, "But don't you do the same thing? Don't you think of me in a certain way sometimes because of how I look?"

It was a truth she'd rather not confess, but since she'd started it, April knew she couldn't avoid an honest answer. "Yes. I'm sorry, too. Except that I do it all the time, with everybody. And I don't fight it the way you do." She drew in a breath. She hadn't meant to be so honest.

Lola laughed. "Well, I'm just a saint," she said dryly. "Anyway, Peter St. John likes you."

April yawned. "He likes you, too."

"No, I mean he really *likes* you."

"Don't be silly!" April said. *Where have I heard that before?* "I'm going to bed. Peter's a nice guy. You can have him."

"He's not a puppy dog, remember?"

"Oh, yeah."

Professor Lowry was uncommunicative all week. April saw *William* once or twice when he was talking with someone else on campus, but she never met *William* herself. Peter and Lola went to the Lakers' game on Friday night, while April sat in the dorm feeling alone and lonely.

When she realized she hadn't eaten since Thursday noon, she went down to the candy machine in the foyer, bought a Snickers bar because of the peanuts, and took it into the lounge. It was empty, but someone had been there because the cover was off the piano. Mrs. Betcher, the housemother, was compulsive about keeping out the dust.

April sat down on the shiny stool and ran her fingers over the keys. "One more thing I can't really do," she told herself as she positioned her hands for *Nola*. Her mother had made her learn just enough to play three or four pieces prettily at a party. She thought of the words "I'm just a bird in a gilded cage," laughed at herself, and played the four songs she knew.

The telephone rang just as she finished. She let it ring six times before she answered.

"Hello. Corman Hall. April Pennington speaking."

"Miss Pennington? This is Professor Lowry."
William?

"I haven't disturbed you by calling at this hour, have I?" His voice was warm and considerate.

William, where have you been?

"I meant to catch you before you left the office."

"No, you didn't disturb me. I was just practicing the piano."

"I didn't know you played." He sounded amused.

There's so much you don't know about me, William.

"I'm wondering if you would drive me to the airport tomorrow. The friend who was to take me has the flu. I got to thinking you might like to use the car while I'm gone."

Oh, William. You thought of me. You really thought of me. "Thank you," April said politely. "I'd be glad to take you."

"My flight is at ten o'clock. Perhaps we could leave early enough to have breakfast on the way."

I don't eat breakfast. "It sounds great," she said enthusiastically. "I'm starving!"

"Forgot to eat again?" He laughed. "I'll pick you up at seven. Good night, Miss Pennington."

"Good night, Professor Lowry." *Good night, dear sweet William.* April put down the receiver, covered the piano, and walked out of the lounge like a dreamer. William was back and he'd thought about her. Of course, they couldn't keep calling each other by their first names. It wouldn't look right. But she wasn't just a secretary to him; she was April. Dear sweet April.

She went straight to her room, sorted through her closet, and picked out a green pantsuit and a tan blouse. Then she sat in front of the mirror, modeling different hairstyles, jewelry, and makeup. At ten, she showered, set the alarm for 5:45, and went to bed to dream of William.

Instead, she stayed awake until Lola and Peter returned from the game at one. *I'm glad they had a nice time*, she thought sleepily as she heard their laughter. *They make a nice couple. We'll have to go out together—William and me and Lola and Peter*. Then as if she'd been a worried mother waiting up for her children to come home, April rolled over and fell fast asleep.

Morning seemed to come only minutes later. The alarm woke her with a sickening shudder through her stomach. Wishing she had more than a Snickers bar to go on, April crawled out of bed, felt her way to the restroom, and splashed water onto her face. Then she stumbled to the toilet, knelt beside it, and collapsed in dry heaves.

The headache would be next. She could feel it coming. She had to get to Lola first while she could still walk. She couldn't let William down. Lola would have to take him to the airport.

When the heaving subsided, April washed her face, wet some toweling with cold water, and pressed it to her head. Then she felt her way down the dark hall to the stairs. Lola's room was in the lower right wing. *I should have asked her to stay with me for the spring break*, April thought regretfully.

Under different circumstances, the boogie man would have tugged at the little girl in April as she descended the staircase to the silent foyer below. Shades of Alfred Hitchcock would have played with her imagination. But this morning a bloody killing would have been an act of mercy.

"Lola!" April reached Lola's door and half-whispered her name, although there was no one else on the wing to awaken. "Lola!"

"April, what is it?" Lola was at the door in seconds. "Come on in. What's wrong?"

The heaves came in waves again, and instead of answering the question, April made for the restroom. She reached the toilet just in time for nothing. There was nothing in her stomach to let go of, but it made no difference to the muscles trying to purge themselves of the nausea.

When April was still, Lola lifted her to her feet. "We've got to get you back to your room before the headache comes, girl," she said gently.

"No, Lola, you've got to help me," April

pleaded, white-faced and panic-stricken. "I promised to take William to Los Angeles Airport this morning. It's too late for him to get somebody else."

"William?"

"Professor Lowry." April ignored the implication in Lola's voice. "Will you drive him to the airport for me? Please."

Lola smothered a yawn. "Of course," she said, guiding April out of the restroom and down the hall to the foyer. "What time?"

"He'll be here at seven." The headache was just minutes away. April knew because colored lights always heralded its arrival.

Lola led her up the stairs. "You still have those pills?"

April nodded. They were in her top drawer with her underwear, but they probably wouldn't help. Nothing really helped her migraines except to live through them. On the other side of it, simple things would seem much sweeter until she gradually took them for granted again.

When they reached her room, Lola helped April back under the covers and stood beside her bed in silent concern. Then she asked, "Have you seen the colored lights yet?"

April nodded.

"Where's the pills?"

"In my top drawer." April rolled on her side and watched Lola through one eye. It felt like her freshman year all over again. She'd had a headache every few weeks that year, and Lola had nursed her without complaint every time.

Maybe we should room together again next year, she thought as Lola went for water. Soni was a status symbol, the most popular girl in the sophomore class. Lola was familiar. Right now *familiar* had a lot going for it.

"I'll check in on you when I get back," Lola said when April had gulped down the pill. "Don't go anywhere."

April tried to laugh. "Thanks," she said, wanting to reassure Lola that she'd be all right. "I was going to a party, but I'll wait for you."

The door to her room shut quietly, and before the pain came, April wondered if she was taking advantage of Lola. William could have called someone else or driven himself and parked the car. In her haste to please him, she had sent Lola off without considering the alternatives.

I'll do her laundry to make it up to her, April thought, smiling as she remembered how Lola hated the task. Then a blinding headache wiped the smile from her face.

CHAPTER
TEN

The headache was shorter than some, but more painful than others. Lola returned from the airport before noon and tiptoed into April's room to find her moaning softly from the pressure that threatened to split her head. Lola placed the car key on the dresser, opened the top drawer for another pill and made her take it, then went for an ice pack.

"Professor Lowry says he hopes you feel better soon," Lola whispered as she placed the pack on April's forehead. Then she rubbed her shoulders and head until April drifted into an uneasy sleep.

The pain disappeared sometime during the night. April wasn't aware of its leaving, only of a sun-kissed meadow that appeared in its place. In her dream, she stood on the grassy slope of a mountain that fell away to a small wooded plateau below.

Mountains ringed the plateau in every direction. The woods skirted it on all sides. But from where she stood, April could see a meadow in the center of it. It was a pastoral scene, something from a book on the early American settlers.

As she watched, a slender woman emerged from a wooden cabin—almost hidden by tall oaks—to call three children who were splashing in the duck pond. As the woman called, a muscular man swung an ax on a huge log, quickly split it into firewood, and then swooped down on the duck pond, loading the children in his arms and carrying them into the cabin.

April was too far away to hear voices or observe expressions, but it gave her a feeling of unqualified domestic bliss. She wanted to run down the mountain, to exchange places with the woman in the log cabin, to be forever a part of that perfect little world.

"You OK, girl?" Lola's voice sounded from far away. "You must be. You've got a smile on your face."

April opened her eyelids a fraction. Lola was dressed for church. "What time is it?" she asked weakly.

"Nine o'clock." Lola smiled. "You've been sleeping your little heart out."

"What church?" April sat up slowly and rubbed her eyes. Lola regularly church-hopped.

"Yours." Lola sat down carefully on the La-Z-Boy. "Peter asked me to come. They're having a meeting after church for people who are interested in going to Mexico this week. Tuesday through Friday."

April raised her eyebrows.

"Yeah, I'm going." Lola studied her sandals, and April thought that it must be warm out again. "I'm just a sucker for a pretty face, I guess." She looked up as if to say, "Tell me I'm a fool."

Not on your life, April thought. *I won't even hint of a "looks judgment" after last week's talk.* "Don't say that," she said seriously. "If you're attracted to Peter, it's for good reasons. Not just because he's good-looking. Anyway, you never can tell what's under a beard."

Lola seemed startled at the thought. "I guess you're right," she said happily. "Right on both counts. I'll see you this afternoon and tell you all about my morning with Professor Lowry."

Their freshman year as roommates, April had been afraid Lola would guess her feelings for Professor Lowry. She'd prevented it by dating often and entertaining Lola with the details. At the time, Lola had been innocent of the ways of men and had listened with the rapt attention of a schoolgirl.

As the year went on, she'd begun to question April's behavior, however: "You shouldn't lead a guy on like that if you aren't serious about him," and "Do you think you're really being fair?" Finally tired of the lectures, April had begun saving her dating tales for Soni and others with similar viewpoints.

Lola had her first date in January of their

freshman year. To April's surprise, he was an upperclassman and a basketball player. To her further surprise, they dated regularly and developed a "serious relationship" that lasted until Mike graduated.

Now when April realized she'd given away her feelings for William, she wasn't sure how to feel about it. On the one hand, she was programmed to dread the moment Lola found out. Lola was sure to say sensible things like, "He's years older than you," and "It's against the rules for faculty to date students."

On the other hand, it would be nice to have someone to talk to about William. And if Lola said sensible things to her about him, she would just say sensible things back about Peter.

Thinking that she finally had a weapon to keep Lola in line, April bathed, dressed, and drove to the neighboring town of Santos for breakfast. It was important that no one recognize her and assume she was skipping church. She felt as if she'd never been so hungry before, and she wanted to savor every bite without guilt.

As she sipped creamy coffee and waited for her omelet, she wondered what to do with the coming week. "Last week was so boring—the research part—that I should make up for it. Especially since I have a car," she murmured to herself.

The waitress bustled over to refill her cup, apologizing for the delay. April blushed as she realized her self-talk had been misconstrued again. "Ladies don't talk to themselves," her mother had said again and again as she tried to break April of the habit.

"You don't want people to think there's something wrong up here, do you?" She would point to April's forehead.

"No, mother," April would say, but she had secretly clung to the habit the way some children cling to their favorite blankets or their thumbs. It was all so strange and frightening— all these rules about being a lady—and she had just wanted to go back to the swinging and climbing days when nobody seemed to care.

"Poor Autumn," April had told her sister on the day before Little Miss Day School. Autumn was only five and didn't know about being a lady yet. "You'll only be free until you're seven."

Margaret Pennington had an epochal theory of raising children. "There are three seasons in the life of a child. Don't send them to school until their seventh birthday," she would say. "Let them alone to develop their own personalities."

All of her theories were tidy. "The second season—from seven to fourteen—is to mold young ladies and young gentlemen. Do it vigorously. Spare no expense. The third season— from fourteen to twenty-one—is to point them toward their civic duties. Be relentless. You'll never be sorry."

April wasn't sure how her mother had developed this philosphy, who or what had influenced her unique perspective. Her mother had a pet philosophy for every occasion, most of them equally bewildering if April stopped to think about them.

In any case, her mother's philosophy for raising children seemed to have worked to her satisfaction. April and Autumn were both sweet young ladies, headed for a life of civic involvement (as wives of prominent men in the community). The only real stir either of them had caused was April's decision to attend King's College.

April hadn't understood the fuss until she'd overheard her mother telling a friend, "I'm afraid she'll become a missionary. That school turns out so many, you know." She realized her mother had accepted her Christianity so easily only because it hadn't threatened her plans for April's life.

The cheese omelet with a cinnamon roll and orange juice arrived. Wanting to stretch out the pleasure of eating it, April took tiny bites and returned to thoughts of her mother. The real reason April had picked out King's College was a postcard of it.

Perched on the California coastline, it had looked so green and peaceful that it had made her want to be part of the peace and greenery. It hadn't been a reason she could defend. Instead, she had gathered proof of its academic standing and insisted she was old enough to choose the school she wanted.

Much later—when there were two thousand miles between her and Chicago's north shore—she wondered if the main allure of

King's College was those two thousand miles. Not that it had kept her mother from showing up unexpectedly. Margaret Pennington thought nothing of jetting out to California for the weekend. But it did mean her mother couldn't move in.

April hadn't seen her mother since Christmas. With both girls in college, her parents had decided on an extended tour of Europe. At first, knowing her mother wouldn't show up unannounced that semester, April felt naked, vulnerable yet full of possibility. With time, she began to miss her parents, looking forward to seeing them in the summer.

She'll call the minute she gets my letter, she thought now, biting into the cinnamon roll. She had finally sent off a short note to her parents, explaining that she'd stayed on campus to work for Professor Lowry, but leaving out the details. It had been impossible to explain how she felt.

Not that her mother wouldn't approve. What college professors lacked in wealth, they made up for in education. William Lowry would make a fine son-in-law. It was just that she couldn't get her feelings out on paper. Nothing she wrote sounded right when she read it back.

The restaurant was growing busier. April wanted to linger over another cup of coffee, but people were waiting to be seated. Instead, she left the expected tip, used the restroom, and drove back to Corman Hall. Lola would be home soon to tell her all about William.

As she parked his white Chevy in front of the dorm, she wondered if her parents would give her a car for her nineteenth birthday. She had given strong hints when she was home at Christmas. Freshmen weren't allowed cars on campus—ostensibly because of insufficient parking—but she'd wanted one since her return sophomore year.

"I probably won't need it that much," she said as she climbed the stone steps to the dorm, no one around to hear. "But it will be nice not to beg rides when I do." Anyway, it was a status symbol. One of the few no one could question. And her parents would buy only the best.

CHAPTER
ELEVEN

"It's all set!" Lola breezed into Corman Hall at a quarter past two. "Six of us are going. Three girls and three guys. We're driving down in Skip's van."

"Long meeting?" April had been waiting in the foyer reading *Guidepost* magazines for an endless hour.

"Yeah. We went to lunch together." Lola flopped down beside her. "It's going to be great. A fun bunch of people."

"Anybody I know?"

"Skip Hemmings and Anita Pryor. Peter and me, of course. Then there's this guy named Hunter and his girlfriend, Cherish." Lola folded her legs under her knees. "Can you believe somebody's actually named Hunter?"

"And going with a girl named Cherish?" April smirked and lowered her voice to approximate a soap opera announcer. "Did Hunter hunt her? Is that how they came to be together? And will he cherish Cherish all of his days? Tune in tomorrow for the continuing saga of *Hunter and Cherish Go to Mexico.*"

Lola laughed. "Maybe it's not his real name," she said. "The name's too perfect for him. This guy looks macho to the max, like he eats lug nuts for breakfast. Maybe it's just a nickname."

"Shame, shame. Looks judgment." April clicked her tongue. "You're doing it."

"In this case, I'll forgive myself." Lola bit the corner of her lip and thought for a moment. Then she said slowly, "But who knows? He may turn out to be a puppy dog."

The two girls sat talking about the Mexico trip until April decided enough time had lapsed for her to mention William without seeming overly anxious. "Did Professor Lowry's plane leave on time?" she asked casually.

"You mean *William?*" The glint in Lola's eyes told her this wouldn't be easy. "Fess up." Lola went straight for the gut. "How long have you been carrying a torch for him?"

April wondered if she should lie and decided against it. As long as Lola knew, she might as well know it all. "Since the week I took his class." She said the words quickly, as if Lola might miss their implication if she did.

"Girl, a year and a half?" Lola gave a low masculine whistle.

April hated the sound. "You never knew I was so steady, did you?" A deep frown wrinkled her brow. "Don't tease me, Lola, please. As long as you know, I want to talk about it."

"A year and a half?" Lola whistled again.

"Schwartz!" April wanted to pound her.

"Schwartz?" Lola burst into laughter. "Schwartz? You've never called me by my last name." She backed away from April. "It sounds different when you say it."

She thought for a moment. "I mean I'm so used to you saying, 'Lola,' in that musical little voice of yours. And now that you belt out, 'Schwartz,' it makes me realize what's wrong with my name. Lola—lilting and sensuous name. Schwartz. Need I say more?"

By the time she finished, April was laughing, too. The expression on Lola's face was comical, as if it had never occurred to her that her names clashed. "Why didn't they name you Hilda?" April asked, glad for a break before they talked about *William* again.

"Hilda?" Lola thought it over. "Do I look like a Hilda? Hilda Schwartz?"

April nodded hesitantly. "You're sort of German-looking. Sometimes."

"Sometimes?" Lola surrendered to loud guffaws. "German isn't something you look one day and not the next!" She spread out her arms. "Do I really look like Frau Hilda?"

When the kidding was over, both girls grew serious. April waited for Lola to speak. And Lola, as if unsure of how to start, stared at the floor for several minutes before she said, "OK, let's talk about Professor Lowry. Tell me how serious this is with you."

April told her about Travis Johnson and Frank Wetzel; about coming to King's College sure she wanted a strong, solid man; about meeting William that first week in archaeology class and falling in love with him. As she came to the end of her speech, she dared to look at Lola. Words of protest were already on her lips, and April held up a hand to stop them.

"Don't say it. Don't say any of the *sensible* things. I already know what they are. He's too old. I'm too young. It's just a schoolgirl crush. This is real life, not the movies." April covered her face with her hands, extending her thumbs toward her ears. "I'm not going to listen if you say things like that."

"OK, I won't say any of the old clichés." Lola reached over to pry April's hands from her eyes. "I'm tempted, but I won't. I'll just accept that you're crazy in love with a man in his thirties."

"So did his plane leave on time?"

"It left on time."

"Did you have breakfast together?"

"We had breakfast together."

"And?"

Lola stood to pace about the foyer. "He said he wished you were there," she said at last.

April pressed a hand to her chest to calm her heart. "See, at least he enjoys my company," she said. "We went to Santa Barbara together last Sunday. He liked being with me. I know he did."

Lola stood motionless by the window, her back to April. Then with a sigh, she turned and walked heavily to the sofa, sitting down beside April with the air of one who must break bad news, but didn't volunteer.

"He thinks you're 'charming,' " she said, taking April's small hands between her large ones and looking her in the eyes. "That Sunday with you stirred feelings in him. It reminded him of when he first met his *wife*. He said the day began innocently enough, but that he should have ended it when he realized how much he was enjoying your company."

"His wife?"

Lola nodded. "He's been avoiding you all week, April, not knowing what to do. Then he decided to ask you to breakfast and explain that he felt his conduct on Sunday had been unprofessional."

"His ex-wife?"

Lola shook her head. "He has been separated from her, but they aren't divorced. She's in England. I guess only a few people at the college know. He didn't tell me until I told him I thought you had a crush on him and scolded him for feeding the fire."

"Does he still love his wife?" April's voice was small and shaky.

"Yes. She requested the separation to 'find herself.' He's been waiting for her. He said that Sunday with you made him realize he should go see her."

"How long have they been separated?"

"Four years."

"That's a long time." April took a moment from her own grief to feel for Professor Lowry's. "And he still loves her?"

"He still loves her." Lola squeezed April's hand. "You're right. He's a good man. Strong and solid. And it's not stupid to be in love with him, but it's impossible."

"That's what Susie Johnson said when I asked about her and the professor." April's lower lip began to quiver. "Why did this happen to me, Lola?" Tears slipped down her cheeks. "I mean, why did Sunday have to happen? It was such a perfect day."

Lola put her arms around April and let her cry, pouring out the tensions of the previous week. "I kept wondering," April sobbed, "does he care or doesn't he? Is it possible or isn't it? Am I brave or stupid to hope?"

When the tears were over, she rested against Lola's comfortable shoulder and thought, *It could have been worse. He could have hated me. I could have made a fool of myself. As it is, I had a beautiful day with a wonderful man. It's something to treasure for the rest of my life.*

"They should have traffic signs on men to avoid collisions like this," she said as she backed away, wiping her face with the back of her hands. "Danger. Look out for broken hearts."

Lola watched April closely. "I told him he should let students know he was married so they wouldn't go around falling in love with him," she said. "He said it would cause too much gossip about why his wife wasn't with him. He said Sunday was the first time he'd slipped up and given a student cause to think he was interested."

"Slipped up?" April smiled sadly. "Why with me?"

"Because you're so irresistible," Lola kidded.

"No, really. Why?"

"I guess God wants you to learn something." Lola stood to stretch and reached to pull April to her feet. "What you need right now is a good run around the track. Go put on some sweats. I'll meet you back here in five."

There she goes, talking like a jock again, April thought as she climbed the stairs to her room. But the old irritation was gone, replaced by a new softness for her old roommate. *God wants me to learn something. But what?*

She pondered the question as she undressed and splashed cold water on her face to soothe her reddened eyes. *What could God want me to learn from having my heart broken?* But as she pulled on a pair of pink sweatpants, she realized to her surprise that she didn't feel like a broken-hearted woman.

She felt sad and quiet and drained of any great emotion, but she didn't feel hopeless the way one should when a love is over. And as she slipped on her Nikes, she wondered if Professor Lowry had been a smokescreen, a safe, wonderful person to be in love with so she wouldn't have to worry about the Travis Johnsons and Frank Wetzels of King's College.

CHAPTER
TWELVE

April asked Lola to spend the night in her room. Ordinarily she would have wanted to be alone, to sink to the depths of sorrow, sure no one else could understand. But this experience was different.

In a subtle yet certain way, she already knew she'd only been in love with the idea of William, not with Professor Lowry himself. And she wanted to talk about it. She wanted to sit up late, pop corn, and let Lola help her sort it out.

The two girls fell asleep at three, better friends now than they'd ever been, and were roused at ten the next morning by a loud banging on the door. "April, is Lola in there?" Kathy Cummings yelled from the hall. "I've looked everywhere, and if she's not in there, I'm giving up."

April rolled out of bed and staggered to the door. "Don't shout," she mumbled as she unlocked the door and opened it to peer into

Kathy's wide face. "Why do you need Lola?"

"I don't." Kathy pulled away with a *humphing* sound. "I've already wasted my life looking for her. But Mike does."

"Mike?"

"Mike Schuster, her love of last year. He drove *all night* to get here, and he's crazy to see her." Kathy *humphed* again.

"I'll get her up," April said, too groggy to understand the significance of Kathy's news. "Tell him she'll be down."

Lola's head was buried under two pillows. April pulled them off and poked her on the arm. "Hey, Lola, get up," she said, beginning with a whisper and moving to full voice as she realized what she was saying. "Mike's here! He drove all night to see you!" Taking in Lola's tousled hair and sleepy face, she added, "Hurry up! He can't see you like this."

Lola stretched and yawned. "Why not?" she said sleepily. "What's wrong with me like this? Tell Mom to come on up."

"Lola, watch my lips." April sat down on Soni's bed and took Lola's face in her hands. "I am going to speak slowly and deliberately," she said, exaggerating her mouth. "Michael Schuster is downstairs. He drove all night from wherever he was just to see you. He has been looking for you for an hour."

Comprehension dawned on Lola's face, only to be replaced by pure panic. "M–M–Mike's here?" she stuttered. "W–why?"

"To see you," April repeated, then added, "and I can think of only one reason for a guy to drive all night to see a girl. Lola, he wants to tell you he still loves you."

"That isn't funny." Lola grasped the covers angrily and pulled them up to her chin. "I haven't heard from him since last year." The look of panic returned. "Tell him to go away."

April shook her head. "I won't let you do it," she said as she opened the shades. "You owe it to yourself to find out what he wants. Maybe he wrote a book about your love affair and wants to give you a cut of the royalties.

"Who knows? The point is you can't send him away without seeing him." She tossed on her bathrobe and opened the door. "I'll sneak over to your room for some clothes while you hop into the shower. Shampoo your hair and I'll blow-dry it for you. If you aren't in there when I get back, I'll . . . I'll do something drastic."

With a final "I mean it" for emphasis, April closed the door and raced down the hall to the fire escape. By using it, she could sneak down to Lola's room, choose something for her to wear, and sneak back without attracting Mike's attention.

Lola's closet was a disaster. The few clean clothes that still hung from the rod were in danger of drowning in the sea of dirty things below. *There's nothing here*, April thought at first. Then realizing Mike hadn't been attracted to Lola for her fancy wardrobe, she picked out a pants outfit, found some clean underwear in a drawer, and fished a pair of sandals out from under the bed. *I hope Lola gets rich*, she thought as she headed back to the fire escape, *because she definitely needs a maid*.

Lola was in the shower when she returned, obediently washing her hair. Within twenty minutes, April had combed and dried it, coaxed Lola into a little makeup, and sent her off.

"Be nice," she said, kissing her on the forehead like a mother sending a daughter off on her first date. "Don't let me down."

April spent the rest of the morning in her room, cleaning and sorting, but mostly waiting for Lola. In her excitement over this mysterious development in her friend's love life, she almost forgot her own disappointment in love.

When Lola hadn't returned by two o'clock, she took a beach towel to the front lawn and napped in the sun.

Lola found her in the library that evening, curled up in a corner with a copy of Daphne du Maurier's *Rebecca*. April had picked it out because she'd read it before and knew she wouldn't be disappointed. "We just got back," Lola said, out of breath from running. "I've been looking all over for you."

"Sounds familiar." April smiled and put the book down. "Where'd you go?"

"To the beach." Lola grinned, a silly half-smile.

"Was I right? Is he still in love with you?"
Lola nodded.

"You're blushing!" April realized her friend was flushed from more than the run and clapped with delight. "You're still in love with him, too, right?"

Lola just kept grinning.

"So why hasn't he called you? What's been happening? Tell me everything!"

"I will, I will, but first help me solve something." A look of concern replaced the sheepish grin on Lola's face. "Mike wants to spend the week here with me, but I've already agreed to go to Mexico with Peter. April. . . ."

Before Lola finished her plea, April knew she would go. There was no reasonable excuse not to, and besides, Lola had been a true friend the past few days. April wanted to be the same kind of friend in return. "Of course, I'll go to Mexico for you," she said immediately. "Don't look so surprised. You went to the airport for me, didn't you?"

"That's a little closer," Lola said.

"It'll be good for me." April stood and walked to the water fountain. "I could use a change of pace," she said, looking back at Lola.

"The orphanage is out in the boonies." Lola followed her. "You'd better think about it before you agree. You'll have to dress down."

"I can dress down!" April glared at her with indignation. "I've been to camp. That does it! Nothing can stop me now."

"You're a good person." Lola hugged her. "I'll pick up the pieces when you get back. Come on, and I'll show you what not to pack."

"Only if you tell me about Mike first."

The two girls walked arm in arm to Corman Hall, whispering and giggling as Lola told April how Mike had resisted the temptation to call her for so long because he was afraid of marriage. Then finally the desire to see her had overwhelmed him until he couldn't think of anything else. A quick call to the college had told him Lola was on campus and rather than risking a phone call he'd simply jumped in his car and driven all night.

"So where is he now?" April asked as she opened the door to her room. "Conked out on the front lawn?"

"I got him a room over at Semples Dorm." Lola walked to April's closet and opened it. "This neatness is disgusting, Pennington," she said. "Remind me to look for a cure."

"Sure," April mumbled, not really listening. She had stopped in front of the mirror and was studying her face from every angle. "Look at me now," she commanded, sitting down at the dressing table. "This is me with makeup, OK?"

"OK, that's you with makeup. So?"

April opened her jar of cleansing cream, dipped in a cottonball and quickly removed her makeup. Then she swung around to face her friend. "So how different do I look without it? A lot or a little?"

Lola thought for a moment. "I'd say in the middle, between a lot and a little. I mean, your face doesn't completely go away like Shannon Price's, but you do look different. What is this? A test?"

"Hang on." April moved to her closet and

took out a plain red T-shirt. Then she found a pair of older blue jeans and changed her clothes. "OK. How's this?" She stood back for Lola to see. "No makeup. No pretty clothes. No jewelry."

"The nails." Lola motioned toward April's long pink nails.

"I can fix that." April found a bottle of polish remover and swabbed the paint from her fingernails.

"The feet," Lola said.

April swabbed her feet, then posed again for Lola's reaction. "What do *you* think?" she asked. "Better? Worse?"

Lola smiled. "Neither," she said enthusiastically. "Just different, but perfect for going to the boonies in Mexico. April, if you go that way, you won't have to worry about how you look. And you won't waste time trying to stay gorgeous." Her eyes flashed a challenge. "Do it if you dare!"

"Of course, I dare!" April put her hands on her hips in mock outrage. "There's more to me than a pretty face. I'm only taking what I can pack in . . . ," she looked about the closet and came out with a small sports bag, "in this bag. Just this and my Bible." She crossed the room to her nightstand and shoved the Bible under her arm. "How do I look?"

"Like Old Maid Maude the Missionary," Lola said with laughter. "Do it, Aprilly. Show 'em how to save the lost."

True to her word, April packed only the basics. Then she soaked in the tub and thought about Mexico. She had never been south of the border, nor had she ever wanted to go. When she thought of it, only poverty came to mind and with it, a depressing hopelessness.

"It's time for me to face some things I've been avoiding," she told herself as she dried. "Mom lives in a beautiful world, but it's time for me to see some of the rest."

She chuckled at the thought of what her mother would say: "Don't you think that's carrying religion a bit too far, dear? People get killed in Mexico. It's too dangerous for a young girl like you."

She grew more serious as she thought for the first time that the trip might have its dangers. Until now, she'd only thought of the inconvenience and the poverty. "I'm not acting like myself, Lord," she prayed as she slipped under the covers. "I hope it's the right kind of different. Lola says you want to teach me something. I guess now's as good a time as any."

Then a peace seemed to fill the space above her bed and gradually descend on her, soothing her anxious thoughts. And as she turned on her side to sleep, she mumbled to the Lord, "I'm glad I'm going plain. I want to see what it's like not to think about how I look."

CHAPTER
THIRTEEN

The alarm clock jarred April awake early the next morning to the unsettling realization that no one had informed Peter of the change in his crew. "Lola says he won't care," April mused as she brushed her hair, "but what if he does? What if he has a thing for Lola? After all, he invited her out."

She had grilled Lola about it the evening before, and Lola had persistently answered, "He likes *you*. I told you before, he *likes* you." But when April had pressed her for how she knew, Lola could only say, "I can tell by the way he always asks about you."

Skip's van was to leave at seven. "Be on time," Lola had warned. "It's a ten- or twelve-hour ride, depending on the stops. Get there fifteen minutes early if you can." April glanced at the Swiss clock. It was exactly 6:15, too early for thinking people to be awake.

She reached for her eye shadow and began to apply it with deft, practiced strokes. It wasn't until she reached for her lip color that she remembered her resolution to go natural. "Do it if you dare!" Lola's challenge returned to her with such force that she grabbed a cottonball and wiped her face clean.

"Amazing how much time you save when you aren't dressing for anything," she told herself as she slipped into the comfortable jeans and shirt she'd modeled the night before. As an afterthought, she braided her hair into two braids, tied them with red ribbons, and let them hang over her shoulders.

"Sunglasses, my Bible, my purse, and my bag. That's it." April checked the room twice to make sure she had everything, then stepped out into the hall and locked her door. "Nothing to worry about." She whistled a little tune as she took the stairs two at a time down to the entryway and out the front door.

Nothing to worry about, she thought. But worry was the first thing she did when she saw Skip's van in front of the ad building. *What if they're disappointed I'm not Lola?* she thought. *What if they don't want me? What if I look ugly? I should have dressed better; a touch of make-up wouldn't have been a big deal.*

She approached the van cautiously, hugging the greenery along the path for comfort. Skip, Anita, and Peter were already there, talking in hushed tones as they loaded the van. "Hey!" Skip turned to wave at her and called out Lola's name. Then he added, "That's not Lola."

April stopped, uncertain whether to continue, and the three stood looking her way until Peter called, "Come on over, whoever you are."

"They don't recognize me," April mumbled as she eased toward them. For a moment, she felt like Godzilla, tracking his way toward the terrified natives. When she reached the group, she put down her bag and waited.

After a silent minute, Anita stepped toward her. "It's April," she said laughingly. "I didn't recognize you with your braids and dark glasses." The two men followed with similar comments.

"I hope you're coming, too," Peter said when they'd established it was really April. "We can squeeze in another body."

"Actually, I'm offering to come instead." April backed away slightly. "Lola has unexpected company from out of town. She asked me to take her place."

"That's a fair exchange." Skip took her bag. "One April for one Lola."

Before April had a chance to hear the other opinions, Hunter and Cherish arrived, distracting attention from her and causing Skip to insist they "get on board right away, and save the small talk for later. It's a long trip."

Hunter and Cherish hopped in first, taking the backseat. April wondered briefly if she'd be paired with Skip or with Peter, but Peter answered the question by taking her arm and helping her into the midsection. "You next," he said, following her into the van as if the seating was his decision. That left Skip and Anita in front.

"Oh, the bear went over the mountain. . . ." Skip broke into camp songs as the van rounded the corner down the main drive. The rest followed, and to April's relief no one talked to her until they were on the freeway.

As she sang, she tried to remember the last time she'd been out in public wearing only her natural face. *I shouldn't feel so naked,* she thought. *But I do.* The only time she could remember was the previous week when she'd greeted Peter in her bathrobe.

"I'm glad you came," Peter said when the singing was over. He lowered his voice. "I even prayed you would."

"You *prayed* I would?" April sounded incredulous.

"Yeah." Peter laughed. "I told the Lord it would be nice if you came along because I wanted to know you better and it would be harder once I got back to UCSB."

Amazed at his forthrightness, April answered in kind. "Why didn't you just ask me out?" she said, watching him behind the protection of her dark glasses.

"You didn't seem exactly interested. I thought maybe you were going with someone. Are you?"

"No, but why would this trip make me more interested?" April held her breath. She'd never had a conversation like this.

"To know me is to love me." Peter puffed up his chest in a false show of ego. "I figured if you were around me for several days, we'd be friends by the time we got home."

"I see," April said, wondering if she should dispute the point. Then she added, "I'm sure you're right. There's no reason for us not to be friends by the time we get home unless one of us does something disgusting."

"I never do disgusting things," he said.

"Neither do I."

"Then it's settled." He put out his right hand. "Shake on it, friend?"

There was a shy silence between them. April broke it by asking Peter about himself. She had learned the best way to relate to boys was to make them comfortable talking about themselves. Peter didn't need urging.

"I was born and raised in Santa Barbara," he said, slouching in the seat and stretching his legs. "I've had a pretty traditional southern California life, I guess. My folks live near the beach, and my brother and I spent a lot of time there. I didn't think about much more than surfing and having a good time until my last year in high school."

He stopped suddenly and stared out the window. "What happened?" April asked carefully when he didn't continue.

"Uh." He looked at her. "A friend of mine broke his neck in the water. I guess it's still hard to talk about. He was the youth minister at our church. A really great guy. All for the kids. He lived for about a week, and when he died, I felt so angry at God I didn't want anything to do with him.

"It was in October and I quit going to church. I quit talking to God, too, but I didn't stop thinking about him. I spent the rest of that year thinking about life and what it means to be alive, what it's all about.

"I decided it was about helping each other, the way Mel had helped us. I decided to work with kids. That's why I'm majoring in psychology. So I can understand what makes them tick."

"How'd you get back with God?" April asked.

Peter looked at her for a long moment, his eyes twinkling. "I think it's impossible to resist him," he said. "He just keeps bugging you: 'Hey, I'm here. What are you going to do about me?' I finally gave in and got over being mad at him.

"Mel's wife was praying for me all the time. I got to thinking that if she wasn't mad at God, why should I be? I started going back to church and talking with God, just kept on from where I left off. I still don't understand why God let Mel die, but I guess I've learned to trust him with it."

The van pulled off the freeway and into a McDonald's drive-through. "I'll pay," Skip said as he took orders, "and you pay me back when we get there."

"If you're so rich, why don't you treat?" Hunter called from the backseat. Everyone laughed, and April turned to look at the couple behind her. Lola had been right about Hunter. April smiled as she imagined him ordering a lug nut McMuffin. He was big and brawny, hairy and handsome in a caveman way.

Cherish, on the other hand, didn't look the slightest like a Cherish. Girls named Cherish were tiny brunettes with faint mustaches on their upper lips. This Cherish was tall and blonde with a crisp, uncomplicated look about her. She turned now to pound her partner on the arm. "Always looking for a free ride, Hunt," she said playfully.

Good. At least, they call him "Hunt," April thought as she faced the front again. Peter reached up to take a bag of McMuffins from Skip. "Sure you just want OJ?" he asked her for the second time.

She nodded. "I'm not a big eater."

"She doesn't scarf food either," Skip said. "If you ever take her to lunch, plan on three or four hours."

He said it in a teasing way, and April felt the color come to her cheeks. She'd gone out with Skip occasionally, and the first time, he had insisted on ordering for her. She'd been unable to eat even half of her food, but rather than appear impolite, she'd picked at it, stretching the evening until closing time at the cafe.

"She looks healthy enough to me." Peter winked at her and pinched Skip on the cheek. "Carrying around a little baby fat? Maybe you should take a lesson from Aprilly and scarf a little less yourself."

"Never." Skip studied himself in the mirror. "My mother likes me this way. She'd never recognize me without my cheeks." He filled them with air to emphasize their chipmunk appearance, then turned to Anita for approval.

"I think you're perfect, sonny," she told him in a high-pitched granny voice. "A mother's dream."

"More like a mother's nightmare," Hunter snorted.

Skip turned on Hunter in good-natured revenge, and when the guys were finished insulting each other, the van was well on its way to Los Angeles. "Thanks for defending me," April whispered in the quiet.

"Anytime, Aprilly." Peter locked his fingers behind his head and closed his eyes, a faint smile on his lips. "Anytime."

So he did it on purpose, April thought with pleasure. She had wondered if it had been intentional or only something to pass the time. *He discovered my nickname, too, without anybody telling him.* This thought pleased her as well. Only her closest friends called her Aprilly, and she realized now that she wouldn't mind including Peter St. John in this category.

CHAPTER
FOURTEEN

Earlier in the day, the group had discussed whether to stop for lunch or to press on toward San Diego for an early supper and a walk on the beach. April had voted for San Diego, but when they stopped by a taco stand for lunch-to-go, she wished it could be for longer than a restroom break.

"I'm driving." Peter handed her a carton of Cokes. "You get the seat of honor."

"Won't Anita mind?" April glanced about the stand for the other girls and realized they were already in the van. She had been with Cherish and Anita in the ladies' room, sharing girl talk about their adventure, but had stayed behind to fix her braids.

"I doubt it." Peter grinned. "I think Skip and Anita have found each other." He pointed toward the van. Skip and Anita were in the middle seat, their heads bowed low in intimate conversation. "It looks as if you're stuck with me," he said.

"I don't mind. I like your company." April arched her back wearily, rotating her neck to work out the kinks.

"Hang on," he said as if he could read her thoughts. "I'll race you down the beach in San Diego. You'll feel good as new."

"How much of a stop will we have?" April followed him to the van, carefully balancing the drinks to keep them from spilling, and waited for him to open her door.

"It's two hours from here if we don't run into traffic." Peter glanced at his watch. "That'll be three-thirty. We can spend a couple of hours, maybe even get some real food." He made a face at the half-eaten burrito in his hand.

Everyone except Peter was asleep within the hour. April glanced through the rear-view mirror before she dozed off and caught Anita and Cherish resting against the boys' shoulders. *It would be nice*, she thought as she leaned her head against the cold door, closing her eyes on a vivid impression of Peter's muscular arm.

Her next impression was of noise and motion, the sounds of friendly laughter about her in the stop-and-go of San Diego traffic. "We're almost here, sleepyhead." She opened her eyes to Peter's smile. "Look. There's the beach." He pointed across her to the bay. "Anthony's OK with you?"

Wonderful, she mouthed. The fish grotto on the water was her favorite restaurant in San Diego, not that she'd been to many others. But shrimp was a favorite, and Anthony's made them just right. "Let's run on the beach first, though." She sat up to straighten her braids and retie her bows.

Peter eased the van down the waterfront, found a parking space a few blocks from the restaurant, and cut the engine. "Are we going together or should we meet here at . . . ," he said, checking his watch again, "five-thirty?"

"Make it six o'clock." Skip brought his arm down from the seat back to give Anita a quick squeeze.

"It's a three- to four-hour trip from here to the orphanage?" Peter spoke the statement as a question, a look of concern on his face.

"Nothing we can do tonight once we get there," Hunter said. "Might as well enjoy ourselves here."

"I'm wishy-washy. You convinced me." Peter hopped from the van to open April's door. "Shall we go, milady?" He flourished a bow, and she laughed at his silliness.

When they were alone, she asked, "Will you really race me?" As she said it, she remembered William and their speeding down the beach toward his white Chevy. *It really was a romantic afternoon*, she thought, without feeling a sense of loss. *I wonder what Professor Lowry is doing now.*

"Are you any good?" They stood at the light, waiting to cross, and Peter pushed the pedestrian crossing buzzer for the second time.

"What?" April, gathering her thoughts, looked up at him in surprise. "What did you say?"

"I asked if you were a good runner." The

traffic halted, and he reached for her hand. "Can you run?"

"I can run. My legs work. I'm not any good."

"OK. Then I'll race you." He squeezed her hand and pulled her across the highway. "I couldn't risk you beating me. Not on our first date."

When they reached the sidewalk, April stopped. "This is our first *date?*" The word seemed foreign to her, as if she'd heard it before but in a different context. "This is a date?" she repeated, wondering why it sounded so strange.

"Well, it's not a–a formal date." He chose his words uncertainly. "But I'd like to think it was something of a date, that if you weren't stuck with me like this and I'd asked you, you would have said yes."

"Of course!" April smiled to reassure him. "Of course I would have. That's not what I mean. It's just. . . ." She was silent for a moment. "It's just that I'm not dressed the way I would for a date. That's all."

"What would you wear?" His voice was curious, and she wondered if he was teasing. They continued down the walk, passing Anthony's and stopping in front of the Star of Hope, an old sailing ship now a maritime museum.

"Do you really want to know?" April asked at length.

"Yes, I do." He motioned to the floating museum. "Have you been inside the Star?" She nodded. "Then let's keep walking," he said. "We'll look for our beach to race on. Tell me what you would wear if this was a real date."

"It's not exactly *what* I would wear," April said. "It's *how* I would wear it. I mean, I would spend a lot of time getting ready. And I would worry about how I looked and if I was dressed right and if you would like it."

Peter stopped. "Yeah?"

"Yeah." April stared up at him, observing his expression to make sure it was genuine and hoping she wouldn't blush. "If I spent so much time getting ready for you, I guess I would feel it worth your spending your time and money on me," she heard herself say. "As it is. . . ." She motioned to herself, thinking her appearance would explain everything.

He studied her for a moment. "You look good to me," he said, "just the way you are. You look great."

"But I don't look special." She added honestly, "This is the weirdest conversation I've ever had with a guy." She looked down at the ground, mentally counting the cracks in the cement square beneath her.

"Aprilly." He said the nickname softly. "You'd look special to me if you were wearing a potato sack." He lifted her chin with his fingertips until she was looking at him. "It's the person inside that's special. Not . . . ," he said, smiling a lopsided grin, "not that I don't appreciate the person outside."

"Do you really think I'm pretty? She backed away from him. "Just like this with no makeup, in these old clothes?"

"I don't even understand the question," he

said, shaking his head in wonderment. A low wall separated the sidewalk from the sea, and he swung his legs over it. "Let's sit for a moment." He patted the cement. "I really do want to understand."

April joined him and soon found herself telling him things she'd never shared with anyone before. She told him about Lola's dare and about coming to breakfast in her bathrobe on her seventh birthday and about Little Miss Day School. When she was through, Peter asked, "You've had lots of boyfriends, right?"

She nodded.

"But you never hung out with any of them? I mean you always went through this business of making yourself perfect before you saw any of them?"

She nodded again.

He gave a short, low whistle. "What a drag," he said as if he could hardly comprehend it. "What a total drag!"

"A drag?" She looked at him questioningly.

"Yeah! A drag!"

The vehemence in his voice caused her to consider his words more than she might have. As she thought about them, she began to agree. "Yeah! A drag!" She repeated his words, using the same inflection, and they both laughed.

"Aprilly, you should dress for yourself," he said, kicking at the water that lapped the wall below their feet. "If you wake up and feel country, tie your hair in bows and go natural. Whatever. Dress the way you feel. A guy might appreciate one more than the other, but if he really loves you, he's going to love you for who you are inside. And the inside you doesn't change with the weather."

They talked about other things next, about school and home, growing up and choosing what they would be. Peter seemed so real, so different from most boys, that April found herself wanting to listen not simply to make him feel good, but to absorb what he had to say. It made her feel safe and comfortable to hear him share his life. Two hours later when they realized they'd lost track of time, she wasn't surprised.

"If we're lucky, we'll have time to grab a hot dog on the way to the border," Peter said as he swung his legs back over the wall.

April held her stomach and moaned. "Please, no more fast food," she begged. "A plain salad maybe, but no hot dog."

"To each his own. . . ." He sang the words in a warbly falsetto.

April laughed, joining him in an off-key alto. Linking arms, they wove their way down the empty sidewalk, past the silent Star of Hope, through the tempting smells of Anthony's, and across the busy street to the van where Skip and Anita waited wanting to know what they'd ordered.

"Conversation," Peter said lightly. "We dined on the elixir of life, on the pleasantries of each other's company. Now I'm ready for a hot dog."

CHAPTER
FIFTEEN

Hunter and Cherish were late. Peter used the excuse to go for his hot dog, leaving Skip and Anita to wait for them. Four blocks later, April learned he was after hot dogs plural, ordering three with the works to go.

"That's the most disgusting thing I've ever seen," she said as she watched in fascination while he gulped them down.

"Does this mean we can't be friends?" He took a paper napkin and wiped his mouth with dainty, exaggerated strokes. "You said we could be friends after the trip unless one of us did something disgusting."

"What can I say?" April pierced a bit of lettuce with her plastic fork and chewed it carefully. "You really blew that one, didn't you?"

Hunter and Cherish were waiting when they returned, but it was dark by the time they crossed the border. With Skip driving his van across, April and Peter were in the middle again. Unaware of her action, she reached for his hand as they passed from the American side into Mexico.

"Afraid?" he whispered, accepting her hand with a small squeeze.

"What?" Realizing what she'd done, April felt the color rise to her cheeks. "A little," she whispered back. "My mother says things. You know, terrorists and stuff like that." She wanted to tell him she was also afraid of the poverty, of the hopeless way it made her feel, but she couldn't admit it until they were alone.

"Don't worry." He pulled her close. "I'll be your personal hero." He rolled his eyes in a ridiculous fashion and she laughed. "Me macho Zorro scare bad hombres away."

"OK, buddy, now tell me which way," Skip called back. "In fact, trade places with Anita until we get through Tijuana. I'm lost on these streets."

"Never fear, Peter's here." Peter took the front seat. "I know my way, sort of."

In reality, he knew the way through Tijuana well, guiding them to the road to Ensenada without difficulty, even in the darkness. When he was by her again, April asked how often he visited the orphanage. "I don't know." He scratched the top of his ear. "Lots, I guess. I started coming down after Mel died."

"When you didn't believe in God?"

"Yeah. It made me feel good, like I was giving something back to life instead of just taking from it. I've been coming down ever since." The moonlight shone through the window, lighting a happy glow on his face. "I can't wait for you to meet the kids, Aprilly. You'll love them and they'll love you."

She reached for his hand again, and he accepted hers without question. "Poverty scares me," she whispered. "I don't know if I'll be any good with your orphans."

"You'll be wonderful," he whispered back. "It scares you only because you're thinking in terms of have and have not. You have things, and they don't have things. But when you get there and you're with them, you forget about things. They have love and you have love. Pretty soon, you just forget about things and think about love."

The road from Tijuana to Ensenada was straight and well paved. April glanced at the speedometer and was surprised to find they were doing fifty-five. She expected to bump-bump down a dusty road all the way. As the countryside flew by, indistinguishable from the States by what she could see, April mulled over Peter's words.

"Pretty soon, you just forget about things and think about love." *That's what Jesus is all about,* she thought. *He's about love instead of things.* And she remembered the night she had decided to call herself a Christian, the intentional kind.

It had been in the summer between eleventh and twelfth grade. A friend had invited her to camp and she'd gone, mostly because her mother was against it and she needed something safe to demonstrate her rebellion. All week she'd been puzzled by the girls in her cabin. Instead of the usual vying for position, there had been a helpfulness and cooperation so foreign that she had been at a loss to respond.

On the last night of camp, April had asked her friend for some time apart to talk. "I can't figure these girls out," she had confessed. "They don't seem real. I've been trying to figure out what game they're playing, but still I don't get it. I can't understand what they're up to."

"April." She had heard the exasperation in her friend's voice. "I've been trying to tell you. They aren't up to anything. There's no game. All of them are Christians, just doing their best to be like Christ."

"I'm a Christian, too," April had responded feebly. "I mean I'm not a heathen or anything."

"I know," her friend had said, "and I'm not saying this to make you feel guilty. It's just that there are two kinds of Christians. There are sort of general Christians like most people in this country.

"And then there are intentional Christians, people who talk to Jesus every day and make him the most important person in their lives. The girls in the cabin belong to the second type. They are intentional Christians. It doesn't mean they're perfect, but it does mean they are more concerned about love than about status. . . ."

April had been resting against Peter's shoulder, and she backed away slowly now to see if he was asleep. She found him looking down at her, a silly grin on his face. "I went to camp between eleventh and twelfth grade," she said, deciding to ignore the fact that he'd been staring at her.

"I came home and told my mother I was an intentional Christian. I think I understood then what you've been saying. About forgetting things and concentrating on love. But it seems as if I've forgotten it.

"I had an experience recently, something pretty devastating." She stopped to consider the truth of her words because the loss of William no longer felt devastating. The word *what* came to his lips, but she silenced him by whispering, "I'll tell you later. It's embarrassing."

Then she went on. "But when it happened, Lola said the Lord was trying to tell me something. I wonder if he was trying to remind me about what's important." She sighed and rested her head on his shoulder again. "Sometimes I think life's too complicated."

"I know it is." He rested his chin on her head. "That's one of the reasons we need God so badly."

It had been a long day, emotionally intense, despite the lack of physical activity. April folded her arms and yawned, not bothering to stifle it. *Bad manners,* she thought lazily, picturing the lecture Miss Dela at Little Miss Day School would have given her.

She had dozed off when Peter nudged her. "Ensenada's coming up," he said. "You'll like it. It's a lot better than Tijuana."

"Better?" she murmured. "Nicer?"

"Nicer. Still a tourist trap, but not as much. Sit up. The shops are still open."

"Can we stop?" April sat up eagerly. "Can we shop?" She giggled. "Can we stop to shop?"

"Only nine o'clock." Hunter's deep voice came from behind. "How about a half-hour pit stop?"

"I need a potty stop," Cherish said, "and that's not negotiable."

"It's an hour's drive from here to the orphanage," Peter warned. "We'll be late."

"Already are." Hunter leaned over the middle seat to emphasize his point.

The group decided on a break from the drive. "Just a manzanita and a couple of shops," Skip promised before Peter agreed. "We'll stick together this time."

The air was crisp, and April gladly breathed in the salty ocean smell as they strolled by little shops to a restaurant on the corner. There she had her first manzanita, the apple-flavored Mexican soft drink that matched the night.

"It was delicious," she told Peter as he guided her back out to the street. "Can I have another?"

"And another and another?" He laughed. "You had two. The better part of wisdom is knowing when to quit. Ask Skip."

It was chilly, colder than before, thanks to an evening breeze kicking up off the ocean. April hugged her arms in an unsuccessful attempt to keep back goose bumps. Noticing, Peter drew her into a shop adorned with leather vests and purses. "Find a poncho you like," he said. "I'm rich and in the mood for giving gifts."

"Really?" April saw the ponchos hanging in the back behind a shelf of glazed pottery. "Define rich." She wanted to choose something in his price range.

"Twenty to thirty dollars." Peter took a white and yellow one from the rack and held it under his chin. "Do you like this one?"

"Not on you. It's a bit frilly." April took it from him. "Here, I'll model and you pick." She tried on several, and Peter chose a beige one with delicate blue flowers.

"I like it," she said happily as she wore it from the store. "I really like it. You have good taste, Peter St. John, for someone who wears big bow ties with yellow chickens."

True to their promise, the group was back in the van by nine-thirty, out of Ensenada by a quarter of ten, and on their way to the small village of Las Casas. As the road grew steadily worse, Skip pulled over to the side. "Anyone want to give it a try?" he asked. "Maybe somebody else can miss those potholes I can't seem to avoid."

"I'm a pretty good driver. Cherish and I'll move up front," Hunter said. "It's our turn anyway."

"I don't remember it being this bad," Peter told him, unbuckling his seatbelt to open the side door and peer outside. "It looks like Tyrannosaurus Rex has been trampling this road. But you can't miss the town. Just keep going straight."

In the shuffle that followed, April and Peter landed in back. "Will you be offended if I lie down?" April asked as the van began to move again. The backseat was wider than the middle and seemed to be tempting her to make use of it.

"I'll even give you a pillow." Peter belted himself in and stretched so she could rest her head on his leg. "I'll be your seatbelt," he said, putting his arm across hers. "Shall I sing you a lullaby?"

April closed her eyes and smiled in the dark. *You're a nice person, Peter St. John,* she thought. *A very nice person.* Then as she faded into sleep, a sickening crunch of metal against metal jarred her back to the night.

CHAPTER
SIXTEEN

A piercing scream followed April, floating uneasily above the silent darkness that enveloped her. She asked about it as soon as she regained consciousness. "Who screamed? Someone's hurt," she said, turning one way and then the other on the high, narrow platform. "It's so light!" She closed her eyes against the glare.

"April! I thought you'd never wake up!" Peter's glad voice floated to her as if he were in another room, but when she opened her eyes, this time shading them with her hand, she found him sitting beside her.

"Where am I?" Her voice was weak and low.

"At Scripps Memorial Hospital." He waited for a moment. "You're in the emergency room. We've been waiting for you to regain consciousness."

"I thought Scripps was in San Diego," she said, unable to comprehend his words. "When did they move it?"

He laughed and reached for her hand. "It's

still in San Diego, silly. And so are you. We were in a car crash yesterday evening. You blacked out on us."

"Oh." April found the information vaguely interesting. "Is everyone all right?" she asked, falling asleep.

"Wake up," a deep voice commanded. "We don't want you to sleep right now." April wondered if she was on a ship with Captain Bly, perhaps in the middle of the ocean.

Peter's voice followed, gentle and caring. "Wake up, April. The doctor wants you to stay awake. You've been asleep too long."

Why should I wake up? she thought. *Sleeping is such a good idea.*

"We've lost her again," the rough voice said. "Next time she comes to, call me immediately."

I can 'come to' any time I want, April thought, *I've done this before. I know how. But I won't do it for you. Maybe you're a doctor, but I don't like the way you talk. If Peter asks me to wake up again, I'll do it.*

True to her word, several hours later when Peter's voice reached her asking her to wake up, April fought against the darkness and opened her eyes. This time the emergency room didn't seem so foreign or so bright. And she awoke with the understanding that she had been in an accident, somehow transferred without her knowledge from the backroads of Mexico to the modern facilities of Scripps Memorial Hospital in San Diego.

A hundred questions came to mind, and she wanted to talk to Peter, to ask him about the others and what had happened. But the doctor with the rough voice descended, accompanied by a horde of nurses, and it seemed as if a lifetime passed before she was alone with Peter again.

"I just want to go home," she said when the last nurse left, pulling the curtains around them and shutting out the emergency room beyond. April reached for Peter's hand. "Let's go back to the college."

He bent his head until it was level with hers. "You've been unconscious a long time," he said. "You can't just rush off after what you've been through."

"What have I been through?" She motioned for a pillow to prop her head. Then she smiled, reassuring him that she was ready to talk. "I feel kind of dazed, and my head hurts a little, but that's all. And it's mostly from being interrogated by Attila the Hun."

"His name is Dr. Arnold, but his bedside manner does leave something to be desired," Peter agreed. "Still, you haven't been unconsious for sixteen hours just because you didn't get enough sleep last quarter."

"Sixteen hours?" She looked at him in surprise. "What time is it, of what day?"

He glanced at his watch. "It's three o'clock on Wednesday afternoon," he said slowly.

"Ohhh Kaaay." April thought it over, adjusting to the news. "So what happened? Was it a drunk driver again?"

He nodded. "Again?"

"No wonder I felt as if I'd been through this

before. I have. My senior year of high school."
April laughed a dry crackling sound. "They say
lightning never strikes twice." She closed her
eyes. "Want to hear about Frank Wetzel's
chin?"

"Of course." His voice was tender.

"Good!" April opened her eyes and sat upright, grinning and thinking it strange she
should feel so happy. "I'll tell you about my
devastating experience, too, if you want. Only
first, do you have a picture of you without your
beard?"

Peter fished for his wallet and handed her
his driver's license. "I haven't had the beard
that long," he explained. "Which do you like
better?"

She studied the likeness, surprised to find
that his chin was dimpled, but pleased to see it
was firm and strong. "I like them both," she
said at last, handing it back. "You look handsome both ways."

He stood to stretch and take a bow. "Thank
you, thank you, thank you." He bowed again.
"No applause is necessary. Just throw money,"
he said grandly, as if onstage before a crowd of
fans. Then after moving the chair from the bed
a few inches, he sat back down. "Now what
about your first accident and this Wetzel guy's
chin?"

"Actually, it was his lack of one." April
launched into her true confession. As she
talked, she was aware of a crisis beyond the
fabric walls of her cubicle, but though she felt
sorry someone was in distress, she felt glad Dr.

Arnold and his nurses were busy somewhere else.

When she finished telling Peter about her first accident, he told her about her second. "We were hit from the right," he said. "The driver, about forty years old and drunk out of his mind, came chugging through a stop sign with no headlights. It was an old car and he wasn't going fast, but he planted his front end in Skip's side doors."

Peter stopped his narrative, as if unsure how to continue, and April thought he looked as if he wanted to cry. "Everyone was wearing a seatbelt," he said at last, "except you. When you laid down, I said I'd be your seatbelt. . . ." He coughed and looked away.

"Peter, you can't blame yourself!" she scolded. "That's silly."

"I fell asleep, too." He looked at his hands in a helpless gesture. "We were both asleep. You whammed into the middle seat because you didn't have your belt on. And I wasn't awake to hold you back."

It's crazy to blame yourself, April thought, but she took his hand and only said, "I'm fine. I really am. Don't worry. It just took me awhile to come around." Then thinking she should say something to move the conversation along, she asked, "So how did you get me here?"

Peter explained that they'd taken her to a doctor in Ensenada. But when morning came and she was still unconscious, the doctor had recommended they fly her to San Diego. Peter was busy entertaining her with the details when Dr. Arnold and two nurses reappeared.

"Well, young lady, we're going to admit you."
Dr. Arnold flung open the curtains around the
bed as if this were good news. "Nurse Hoesler
will take care of everything." He took out his
flashlight and reached down to shine it into
her eyes again.

"Why?" April backed away in alarm. "Why
are you going to admit me?"

"Because you've had a concussion. A rather
severe one. Please hold still." Dr. Arnold
frowned with the impatient look of a man who
wasn't used to contrary opinions.

"I don't want to be admitted. I'm going
home." April ducked under the doctor's arm
and slid to the end of the bed. "Peter's going to
take me home." For a moment, she sounded
like a wounded child. Then, realizing it
wouldn't help to appear unreasonable, she assumed a matter-of-fact tone.

"This has happened to me before," she said.
"If there's nothing wrong except a concussion,
there's no reason for me to stay. I mean, there
isn't any medicine you can give me to make it
better. I just need to rest and take it easy,
right?"

"We can't keep you against your will," Dr.
Arnold replied stiffly. "If you were a minor, we
could call your parents. But your chart says
you're eighteen."

"Yes, I am." April slid carefully from the
high bed, and as Peter reached to steady her,
she tried to explain. "My parents are in Europe, and if you admit me, I'll have to call

138

them. They'd never forgive me if I was in the hospital and didn't let them know.

"Since I'm fine, it's silly to worry them and make them come all this way for nothing. Last time I was in an accident, I had broken bones besides a concussion, but I learned then there's nothing to do for a concussion except rest."

"Is she right, doctor?" Peter moved behind her, his hands on her shoulders, and steered her to the chair he'd been sitting in. "What will you be watching her for if she stays?"

Dr. Arnold shrugged impatiently. "Tell him what to watch for," he told the tall nurse, motioning toward Peter, "and then let her go. I can see she'll fight us on this if we insist." Then he yanked the curtains back into place and left.

April raised her eyebrows to say, "See I told you, Attila the Hun," but sat quietly by the bed while Peter took notes on how to watch her for neurological damage from the accident.

"Are you going to quiz me on the presidents of the United States and ask me to touch my nose every half hour?" April teased as he wheeled her through the emergency exit to a waiting cab. She had insisted she could walk, but he had refused to listen, claiming her health was in his hands and Attila would hunt him down for the kill if he blew it.

"Where to from here?" she asked as the cab pulled away from the curb.

Peter put a hand up to smother a yawn. "The Holiday Inn and a good night's sleep," he said, giving in to the yawn. "While you've been out like a light, I've been awake worrying. If you feel good in the morning, we'll take the train home."

"Poor Peter." April snuggled close to him, resting her head on his shoulder. "Who's been looking after you while you've been taking care of me?"

CHAPTER
SEVENTEEN

Peter saw April to her room and then stood in the hall, asking if she was sure she'd be all right. "I'll only be next door," he kept reminding her. "Wake me even if you just get lonely and need somebody to talk to."

At first, April wondered if he wanted to kiss her good night. Then as he delayed, she wondered why he didn't. Finally, she thought it must be that he was shy. Later alone in her room, she decided he was too much a gentleman to take advantage of her emotions after the accident. This thought pleased her, and she went to sleep feeling happy to be near him.

"Is it possible?" April bolted upright in bed, echoing the question to the morning rays that filtered around the heavy institutional drapes. "Is it possible Peter St. John loves me?"

She flopped back on the bed, rolling to smother a giggle in the pillows. She had been dreaming about him. In her dream, they were walking arm in arm through an arboretum.

"Back home in Illinois," she whispered now, "because the trees were in full blaze with autumn colors."

They had stopped on the crest of a hill, admiring the panorama, when Peter blurted out, "I love you, April." In her dream, she had turned to look up at him, and as she did, his nervousness changed to confidence. "I really do love you, April," he had repeated, his voice full of tenderness.

"Silly girl!" April jumped out of bed to look in the mirror. "It's brain damage from the accident. The first president of the United States was Abraham Lincoln. See? You can't even think straight." She touched her finger to her nose, missing it and hitting her cheek. "You're a hopeless case!"

Then laughing a crazy cackle, she ran to the bathroom, turned on the tub, poured some bubblebath from a tiny bottle labeled "Moisturizing Bath Crystals," and sank into the warm foam. Attempting to forget about Peter, she began to recite the Gettysburg Address.

" 'Four score and seven years ago, our fathers brought forth, upon this continent, a new nation, conceived in liberty, and dedicated to the proposition that all men are created equal. . . .' " She spoke the words to the shower curtain, summoning up a dignity unfit for the occasion. Then ending the speech and realizing the Lincoln in her head looked like Peter, she gave up the pretense and gave in to her feelings of delight at meeting him for breakfast.

They had agreed to meet at nine o'clock in the coffee shop downstairs. "I'm hungry enough to eat steak raw," she told herself as she dressed, "and it's the first time I can remember being hungry in the morning."

Peter was waiting for her outside the coffee shop, the morning's paper folded across his knee. He stood as she stepped from the elevator, pleasure lighting his face. "I worried about you all night," he said as he crossed to meet her. "Do I look haggard and worn? I kept wanting to wake you to see if you were all right, But I knew it would only defeat my purpose."

"You look wonderful!" April took his arm. "You look terrific! I love the way you look. And I slept great. The best ever. It's a fabulous day! God's in his heaven and I'm on his earth, thanking him for the privilege."

A waitress in a blue uniform seated them toward the back of the shop. When she was gone, Peter told April to touch her nose. "Who was president before Reagan?" he asked when she completed the task with ease.

"Washington, of course." April laughed at the concern on his face. "You didn't say how much before. Will it make you feel better if I recite them from the bottom up? I'm into history lately." She giggled. "I said the Gettysburg Address in the tub this morning."

"So you're feeling good as in *good*, not giddy as in *giddy*?" he asked, still watching her with caution. "No headache, no dizziness, nothing?"

"I'm feeling *fine*." April tapped the menu for

emphasis. "I'm feeling *great,* better than fine. And I'm *hungry.* I can't remember ever wanting breakfast before."

When the waitress returned, Peter ordered black coffee. April asked for a three-egg omelet, orange juice, and biscuits. As he watched her devour her food, a look of satisfaction replaced his concern. "Anybody who can eat like that has to be in good shape," he said with appreciation.

They chatted through breakfast about everything and nothing, teasing and laughing as if they'd been friends for years. Afterward, there was only time to grab their bags and head for the Amtrak station. It wasn't until they were seated on the train, passing through Del Mar, that their conversation became serious.

"When you told me about your first accident, you said you'd tell me about your 'devastating experience.'" Peter had been looking out the window toward the ocean. Now he turned to April, a relaxed but intent expression on his face.

"You won't laugh? It's embarrassing. I mean it was a true lesson. I think God gave it to me, but it makes me seem pretty dumb." April studied her nails and thought they looked dull without polish. "I thought maybe you'd forgotten that I'd offered to tell you."

She waited, certain he would answer lightly, teasing that he'd never forget anything about her. Instead, his voice was serious. "I guess I just want to know everything about you," he said. "If it was devastating to you, it won't be funny to me."

April looked at him, and for a moment, neither spoke. Then she said softly, "Remember how I'd given up on guys my age by the time I came to King's College? How I said they seemed so phony?"

He nodded. "I remember."

April turned away, hoping he wouldn't notice the color rising to her face, and continued. "Well, I fell in love with an archaeology professor at the college my first week in his class. I should say I *thought* I fell in love, because I know now it wasn't the real thing. But it was a fantasy I lived in for a year and a half. Then just when it seemed to be coming true, it fell apart. I found out it had only been an illusion."

She waited to see if he would say something, but he was silent, still listening. "His name is Professor Lowry. . . ." She went on to tell him the details. "When I asked Lola why this had happened to me and she answered that God wanted to tell me something, my life began to . . . ," April searched for words to finish the story, "shift directions. That's the best way I can put it.

"I've been thinking about it since I found out he was married and wondering why I've been so caught up with appearances. How I look to others, what others look like to me—it's been so important. But those things aren't important to Jesus. I've been calling myself a Christian, but I haven't been taking it to heart."

When she was through, there was a long silence before Peter spoke. April looked to see if there was judgment on his face, but all she saw was sympathy. Finally, he said, "Most of us don't take the Christian life to heart until some experience comes around to shock us into it. I think that's what Lola meant. We mature in stages, and usually not because we want to, but because we have to."

As the California coast flew by, maintaining the illusion trains give of standing still while the world moves, April and Peter discussed life—what's real and how to find it. When they arrived in Santa Barbara, it seemed as if the trip had been either minutes instead of hours or a month instead of a day.

Peter had phoned ahead to ask Lola to meet them. She was waving by the side of the tracks as the train pulled in, a jubilant Mike behind her, his arms around her waist. "They've decided to get married." April nudged Peter for him to hurry. "I'm dying to hear."

"Don't say the word *dying*." Peter dodged a short bald man with too many shopping bags. "After what you've been through, I don't want to hear you say it."

A close look at Lola's face told everything. But Mike, who had been the strong, silent type at school, couldn't stop talking about it. "It's amazing!" he kept saying as they drove toward the college. "I've been sitting on my feelings for so long, afraid to let them come out, and now it seems so right. It's amazing! Of course, we're getting married. I can't figure out why I didn't catch on sooner."

"I've been wondering that about myself," April murmured, but Mike and Lola were too intent on their own joy to hear her. Only Peter understood what she was saying and squeezed her hand to tell her so.

CHAPTER
EIGHTEEN

"How about doubling this evening?" Mike asked as they pulled up to Corman Hall. "You can help us celebrate our engagement."

"I'd love to," April said.

"Tomorrow." Peter put an arm around her. "I promised the nurses she'd take it easy. It's been a long day already. Believe me, she doesn't feel as good as she feels." The car stopped, and he reached over April to open her door.

"If I'm so feeble, maybe you'd better run around and help me out," she said without moving toward the door. "Anyway, you make it sound like I'm two."

"Tonight you're two." He grinned, took her head between his hands, and kissed her forehead. "Now be a good girl and slide out of the car before Uncle Petey has to come haul you out."

"Uncle Petey? I love it!" April made for the door and dragged him behind her, his kiss still tingling on her forehead. For a moment, they stood beside the car, so close she could feel the rhythm of his breathing. She waited, knowing he wanted to hold her, but sure he wouldn't until the time was right.

"I'll walk you to the door," he said finally, taking her bag from Mike and hoisting it over his shoulder.

"Yeah." She turned to Lola. "Thanks for coming. Don't have too much fun without us."

At the door, Peter set the bag down and opened the door for April. "Please get all the sleep you can tonight," he said gently. "I'll call you in the morning."

"OK." She stepped past him. "You, too. Take care of yourself. You're the one who missed a whole night's sleep."

"Good-bye."

"Good-bye."

He handed her the bag and then let the door close. April watched him through the leaded glass as he walked away. "What a wonderful person," she whispered to herself. "Just a wonderful human being." That night as she closed her eyes to sleep, she added, "And a terrific guy!"

Peter called at ten the next morning. "I've been waiting since seven!" April told him, unable to conceal her excitement. *If it scares him because I'm too eager, it scares him,* she thought. *I don't want to play those games anymore.*

"I have to confess something," he said, pausing for her to ask what.

"What?" she obliged.

"I've been waiting to call since five."

"Five?"

"It's a little hard to sleep with you on my mind." He laughed. "I have another confession."

"Two in one day?"

"Actually, there's three, but the third can wait. The second is that I don't want to spend the day with Mike and Lola." He took a breath, and April held hers, waiting. "I want to spend the day alone with you," he continued. "Right now I feel too selfish to share you with anyone."

"How about a picnic?" April suggested, remembering her dream. "We could go to the forest preserve."

"I'll bring the lunch. Pick you up in an hour." He sounded as if the idea was inspired. "Is that all right?"

April thought how completely right it was while she dressed. "I've never felt so free to be myself with another person before," she told her image as she dabbed on violet shadow. She had wondered how to dress and remembering Peter's words, dressed the way she felt. "Soft and romantic." She stroked on a little blusher. "Ready to be loved."

All the way to the forest, Peter was quiet, as if he had something on his mind. April sat beside him, not too close but not too far away on the wide seat, chatting about anything that came to mind. With another date, she would have worried that his silence meant he wasn't pleased with her. With Peter, she felt sure it had a reason he would share when he was ready.

"I dreamed about us the night we spent in San Diego," she said as they spread a beach blanket under a spreading oak. "We were in an arboretum like this." She smiled at the memory. "It was one of those good dreams that make you feel warm and cozy inside."

"What did we do?" Peter looked at her with interest.

"Well, we went walking." April sat down on the blanket and patted the ground beside her.

He dropped down on one knee. "And?"

"It was autumn. We walked through the fallen leaves and admired the colors."

He found a twig and tossed it into a stream that rippled several yards from where they sat. "We held hands as we walked?" He turned to look at her. "Like this." He held out a hand.

"Yes." April put her small hand in his larger one; then watched his fingers close over hers. "We held hands and walked to the crest of a hill."

"And?" He watched her fiercely.

She felt the color flood her cheeks. "We stood there admiring the view and. . . ." Her chest felt tight as if something were pressing against it, cutting off her air. "And. . . ."

"I told you I loved you?" He finished the sentence for her.

She nodded, wanting to look away but unable to do so.

"That was my third confession." He reached

to pull her toward him. "Did I do this?" he asked, bending to kiss her.

She shook her head. "I woke up before you could." Her voice was little more than a whisper.

"Would it have been all right?"

"Oh, yes!"

His lips closed on hers, sweet, tender, and full of promise.

After lunch they walked hand in hand, the way they had in April's dream. And they talked about being in love, about learning to know each other, about being real. "I don't want to waste time pretending around you, Peter," she said as they packed the picnic things. "Next time I'll make the lunch."

"That bad?" He looked hurt. "I thought it was pretty good."

"It was delicious." A smile played on her lips. "I told you so. I'm not taking it back. But I can't even make a good sandwich, and you might as well know it from experience."

April and Peter shared the evening with Lola and Mike, celebrating in Santa Barbara their newfound loves. The evening reminded April of her Sunday with William—dinner, a walk on the beach, the movies, and dessert. "I'm living my life in reverse," she whispered to Lola as they walked into the Bogie festival.

"You know what they say about falling off a bicycle," Lola whispered back. "Get on again and ride."

The next morning, April was waiting for Peter on the front lawn when a familiar voice rang out behind her. "Miss Pennington. I heard you had quite a nasty spill while I was away."

She looked for an escape and, finding none, prayed the ground would open up to swallow her. She hadn't counted on meeting Professor Lowry so soon and so alone. She'd rehearsed it in her mind, but always it was in a crowded hallway where she could greet him impersonally and pass along.

"I hope you're all right." He strode around her and knelt on the grass, his handsome face a picture of sympathy. "First such a terrible headache and then a car accident. You're a walking time bomb!"

April took a deep breath and launched into her reply. "I'm fine, Professor Lowry. How was your trip? I thought you weren't returning until late tomorrow evening. Lola was going to pick you up."

"I know." He sat down and folded his legs. "I cut my trip short to return for my things. I'm taking a leave of absence. There's some . . . ," he searched for words, "business in England I've let go too long." He looked at her questioningly.

"I know." April tried to smile, but her lips quivered. "Lola told me."

"I'm sorry," he said humbly.

"No, it's all right." Touched by the mixture of pain and concern on his face, she rushed to reassure him, her self-consciousness falling away. "It's really OK. I've learned a lot about myself this week."

"As have I." He seemed about to say more, but a shout from the parking lot interrupted them.

"Are you down there, April?" It was Peter's voice.

April turned to look for him and found him standing beside his station wagon. "Yes," she called back. "Come meet Professor Lowry." She turned to the professor. "That's Peter St. John," she explained. "He's a junior at UCSB. I've told him all about you."

Professor Lowry seemed to understand. "I see," he said, smiling. "That's wonderful." He stood and April followed. "Oh, one thing," he added. "Remember the sapphire?"

She nodded.

"I had it set in a band. It's not terribly valuable, but I still think it's rather lovely. Since it's partly yours, I thought I should ask you if you mind. I'd like to take it to England with me."

"Oh, not at all," April replied, a bit too forcefully. She had been afraid he would offer it to her as a memento of their day. "That's a wonderful idea. Please do!"

Peter joined them, and after they had exchanged greetings, Professor Lowry wished them the best and left. "Poor Professor," April said. "Love is all confused and troubled for him. Love is wonderful for us."

"So then it can get confused later." Peter laughed, pulling her close.

"Funny, now I can't imagine being in love with him," she mumbled. "Susie Johnson was right. It would be impossible."

"Maybe we fall in love with impossible people to protect ourselves from possible ones. It gets risky. Still willing to take a chance on me, Aprilly?"

On you and on God, she thought, warmth and happiness flooding her heart.